SAYA LOPEZ
ORTEGA

The Seduction Expert

First published by VSP Publishing, New York, 2019.
ISBN: 978-0-998-42770-6

Printed in the United States of America
Published by VSP Publishing
www.vsppublishing.com

Author websites:
www.sayalopezortega.com
www.facebook.com/sayalopezortegausa
www.facebook.com/theseductionexpert

CONTENTS

CHAPTER 1

Monday, May 1st,
Paris, France

The sun rises in the most beautiful city in France. A ray of light progressively spreads over my face and gently wakes me. I moan, open my eyes, and slowly start to move. This morning, I am having a hard time getting out of bed. I'm delicately wrapped in satin sheets and I'm finding it difficult to leave the comfort of my luxury bedding for the uproar of my professional life. I'm a consultant. A seduction expert, to be precise. Women contact me to take over their love lives. I step in when they're lost, I'm supposed to succeed where they failed. I handle their single status, their relationship, their breakup, and very often their partner's affairs. My job is a life priority and I spend most of my time at the office or between two flights in business class. This morning, like every day for the last five years, I get ready in a hurry and head for one of the biggest consulting firms which I founded.

As soon as I enter the building, I get stares. I'm the seduction expert, everyone knows it and my function intrigues. Women want to call on my services and men imagine life by my side. I daunt humankind and very few people dare approach me. I, therefore, reach the elevators to my office, alone. Upstairs, I find my greatest admirer, my assistant Marie. Marie loves me unconditionally and her life is entirely devoted to me. Of course, I sometimes suspect that she brows dating apps on her lunch breaks, but the rest of her time is fully mine. She picks up my shopping bags, takes my suits to the cleaners, books my tables at restaurants, and each morning, she lovingly rushes to hand me an orange juice, the messages, and the schedule for the day.

"Good morning, Baroness!"

"Good morning, Marie."

"Here's your orange juice, your messages, and your schedule for the day."

"I'm listening, Marie."

"The week's invitations are on your desk, you have a tail in the afternoon, lunch with your tax consultant, a meeting in the morning, and client #5399 is already in your office."

Perfect, she will kick off the festivities. My clients always have fabulous requests and I am always very impatient to see the resulting enthusiasm on their faces. Some have taken out their savings and have waited for months for this first consultation, and our meeting makes them even more overjoyed since they have never seen me. As soon as my office door opens, I become intoxicated from that exhilarating cocktail that they give off and which incidentally pleasantly nourishes my ego.

"Good morning, Aurelie."

Aurelie, client #5399, a number among others.

"Good morning, Baroness!"

"Please, remain seated."

She is sitting on one of the two guests' chairs in front of my office and she scrupulously contemplates me in a long church silence. I likewise sit down in my executive chair and take advantage of her amazement to organize my work tools:

a brushed aluminum laptop, a smartphone, and a stack of clients' files that I carefully put on the tempered glass desk.

"I almost forgot!" she exclaims while plunging her head into her handbag. I raise my eyebrows in surprise. Would there be something around deserving more attention than me? "I'm sorry… would you sign it for me?"

I'm relieved. It's a mini best-seller I wrote. I might add that I'm quite proud of it, I published it anonymously and it got no media coverage whatsoever.

"With pleasure."

I take one of the steel pens laid on my desk and sign the first page with my artist name initials, without adding the slightest affectionate word. My mere presence is often enough to please them.

"I admit I devoured it! Your advice has been so helpful! You're my biggest source of inspiration! I'm so excited about being in your office! And you're so beautiful… could we take a selfie together?"

"Aurelie, appointments are for clients, not groupies. Are you a client or a groupie?"

"I don't know… both!" she assumes, clutching her bible.

"No, you have to choose. If you're a client, behave like one. If you're a groupie, my assistant will have to show you the way out."

"Then I'm a client."

"Will you show some restraint?"

"I can do it."

"Are you sure?"

"Of course, look." She puts my masterpiece back in her handbag. "I'll control myself." I hope for her sake. "I promise!" At the risk that she finds herself kicked out the door. "I'm ready."

Good.

"Today's meeting will let me assess your personal situation. I'll ask you a series of questions and I expect very precise answers. Then, I will propose a solution that will allow you to reach your goals. You're free to accept or decline."

"I'll accept."

"It's a good choice."

The rare ones who refuse always regret it in the end.

"You have all my trust!"

Wonderful.

"So, tell me, what's the target's name?"

"The target?"

"The young man for whom you're here today."

"Oh, Huh, David."

Here she is, as red as my stiletto's soles. That strongly suggests she already imagined a multitude of projects at his side: a stroll along the beach, a declaration, a wedding, a two-story house, four children, and three cars in the garage.

"Tell me more."

She evasively shrugs her shoulders.

"Let's say I like him."

"You like him?"

She strokes her fingers sensually when she speaks about him, but *she likes him*.

"Yes, I like him."

"You call on a seduction expert whose services cost a fortune, for a young man who, I quote, *you like*?"

"Let's say I like him a lot."

"Let's say rather you're madly in love with him."

"If you wish, yes."

"No. You're madly in love with him. Your confession matters, be clear with yourself."

"Okay I admit, I'm in love with him!"

She bites her lip and I take note on my computer that the client presents a slight level of emotional dependency.

"Describe him to me."

"He's blond, tall and athletic." Says the young skinny, short girl, here goes the cruel mismatch. "As a matter of fact, he's very handsome…" In plain English, narcissistic, proud, and presumptuous. "… and single!" she gushes with starry eyes.

Here's at least a point that won't prevent acquiring the target.

"Are you in the same university?"

"We're in the same art history classes."

"How often?"

"Three times a week and there are also evening classes but he doesn't always come."

My fingers play on the keyboard, the notes are pouring in. I notice that they both share the same auditorium, that, even though it's filled with more than five hundred students, remains a potential meeting place. I note that the environment is conducive to interaction, that we'll be able to multiply *eye contact* and increase, exponentially, the desire between the two protagonists. Post scriptum: provided that we can make her desirable.

"Are you in touch?"

"A friend introduced us."

"How do you communicate?"

"We often text or chat on Messenger." What a joy to have to deal once again with the platonic love affairs of a seventeen-year-old kid. "Sometimes, I have the feeling we're flirting, but I'm not sure."

What nonsense.

"At your age, you should be able to put things in perspective, don't you think?"

"Well, I'm not the only girl he compliments."

I hand her a pen and a square sheet.

"Write down your Facebook login." We're going to analyze the psychological profile of this smooth-talker. "You'll also leave me your mobile phone. I'm taking over your text conversations for the next few hours." *Of course not.* "You'll recover it from my assistant in the afternoon. Afterward, you'll go home to primp yourself, you'll have a date with David. Marie will send you the details by text."

"That wasn't the agreement…"

"What was the agreement?"

"I don't know," she chokes while pulling a lock of hair behind her ear. "I thought you'd first help me be more confident."

What for?

"Such coaching would cost you a fortune. I take your financial status into account and save for both of us a waste of time."

"You're catching me off-guard, I wasn't expecting that."

Of course, she was, let's not play naïve.

"That's the reason you came."

"Yes, but I'm not ready for a date."

"I'll come along with you, I often lead dates."

For my greatest pleasure.

"I'm sorry, I won't make it."

"Aurelie, it's now or never. As a matter of fact, it'll happen this afternoon. Marie will give you a list of recommendations to ensure your date's success. Moreover, your lunch will need to be light, neither plentiful nor spicy. The idea is to avoid bloating, gastric refluxes, and gag reflexes."

"I think I'm not feeling so well."

She puts her hand on her heart and takes a deep breath.

"That's normal, your heart rate is increasing. In a few minutes, your cheeks will also be very red." It's the principle of vasodilation, a natural mechanism allowing blood vessels to increase their diameter.

"But why is that?!"

"It's a direct consequence of your heart rate's acceleration, which in turn is linked to your apprehension. But don't worry, Marie will give you a *Fenty Beauty* to hide all that."

"No, no, no, I'm really not feeling well!"

She vigorously pulls on her shirt's collar and frantically waves her hands to create air. I, therefore, decide to close the meeting.

I press the call button linked to my assistant's desk and she enters the room within a minute with her flawless professionalism.

"Yes, Baroness?"

"Marie, take care of Aurélie, please. Give her two Xanax's and forward her file to Sophie."

"Yes, Baroness."

"Aurelie, I'll see you in the afternoon. Don't worry, everything will be just fine."

She leaves the premises as quickly as she got in. Torn between the intense desire of living her fairy tale and the insurmountable fear to face it. As for me, I can easily foresee the disastrous outcome of a students' fling, but to ease my conscience, I still connect to our target's Facebook profile. Obviously, my suspicions are immediately confirmed. His interest in my client has nothing noble. He has many female friends, half of them being tagged on drunken parties' pictures and each of his conversations unveils an aspiring narcissistic pervert. He holds the manners of a perfect heart-breaker and he truly is one. I'll throw my client in his arms, he will psychologically destroy her, she'll fail her finals due to depression, and she'll hold me responsible for her misery that she'll have paid five thousand euros for. A fortune to her, a Burberry trench coat to me. Should I prevent this relationship from happening or give this kid the dream she desires to come true? That's the dilemma I daily face.

CHAPTER 2

Monday, May 1st, 10:00 a.m.

"**B**aroness, the Ingalls are waiting for you in the boardroom."

"Thank you, Marie."

The Ingalls are a whole bunch of redheads with bifocals glasses, who dress in the seventies' fashion. I call them that in reference to Laura Ingalls, symbolic character brilliantly embodies naïvety and innocence. Those young women are confirmed bachelorettes dreaming of a relationship. They're always eager for advice and never hesitate to pull out their credit cards to buy all kinds of coaching services. I, therefore, meet them every Monday in the boardroom, sitting next to each other, gazing at me with lovesick cow eyes, and fiercely clinging to their MacBook.

I always savor these Monday morning meetings. The occasion for me to wear my new dress suits and walk across the room as a TV presenter would. I am well aware of being a role model to these young women and I'm specifically proud of the admiration they display when I enter the boardroom: heads simultaneously turn, hearts pound wildly, pupils dilate, and silence rolls out the red carpet for me.

"Good morning, Ladies!"

"Good morning, Baroness!" they shout all together.

"Reminder of lesson number one: men like proud women. Conclusion: never chase them because you'll lose efficiency. Lesson number two: you must give them a good reason to court you. That reason is your appearance. It's your packaging and your brand image, hence the makeover phase you will undergo this afternoon."

"Forgive me, Baroness…" the least shy of them all suddenly interrupts. " Is the makeover really necessary?"

Given the laughable and pathetic image that they convey to men, it is most of all a matter of survival. Deontology forcing me to adopt more moderate words…

"You're not alone on the market. Competition is fierce, so you need to stand out."

She raises her hand.

"In what way?"

"Look at me," I say authoritatively while placing my hands on my hips.

"I am…"

Her eyes spin around.

"What do you see?"

"The seduction expert?"

"What else?"

"A hot brunette dressing in Armani?"

"What do I express?"

"You're so elegant!" she exclaims with awe.

"Here we are, you must stand out with elegance and subtlety because you attract what you are." Which is nobody, hence the continuity of their bachelorhood. "You're not a woman but the woman." At least… "That's the message you need to convey."

Am I being clear enough? So much hope in the eyes of

those who want to look like me. Are they conscious they'll never succeed? Should I tell them or let life take care of it?

A beep rings.

Marie is on line one.

"Baroness, you have a call from New York."

"New York?" I don't know anyone there, who can be calling me from New York?

"The person says it is urgent."

It seems the question raises enough intrigue to enable me to adjourn this meeting.

"Transfer the call in my office, I'm coming."

"Yes, Baroness."

"Ladies, we are going to have to shorten today's meeting. My assistant will transfer you the information about your makeover session. Meanwhile, I'll let you enjoy the croissants and coffee we've generously set at your disposal."

Their pouts are unequivocal and yet not one of them objects. That only goes to show how weak their personality is.

"Baroness, I have a favor to ask you," one of them suddenly whispers, while standing in the way leading to the door. Needless to say, her audacity deserves attention.

"I'm listening." Without omitting to hit her with my severe scrutiny which make her instantly turn red like a tomato.

"This weekend, I'm having dinner with my parents. I'd like to know if you can find a man to escort me."

"Sure, I have that in stock in my Vuitton."

"You're a seduction expert. I thought it was part of your skills," she says, her voice shaking under fake stoical looks.

"My job is to streamline your interpersonal approach so that in the long term you can manage your own romantic affairs. At the risk of disappointing you, I don't have a gigolos network."

"You've however answered favorably to one of the girls of the group," she blushes, not daring look at me.

"Who's that?"

"Emilie, you've apparently provided a man to escort her to a wedding."

"Indeed, it was an actor. In other words, a paid service."

Nothing more than a strategy to make her ex-boyfriend jealous.

"How is my request different from hers?"

Call the fire department, her throat threatens to burn down.

"The actors that we provide must only allow to improve your image with men, which, in my jargon is a case of force majeure."

"I haven't seen my parents for six months, they really expect good news. Isn't that a case of force majeure?"

"Unfortunately, your family problems are none of my business."

I nonetheless salute the courage it took her to confront me.

"I'm begging you, Baroness, let me keep up appearances."

Keep up appearances… they all want it. They are very worried of the image they convey to their family and going back to their hometown terrifies them. Dinners are genuine inquisitions in which they not only have to admit their single status but also explain it. Which they can't. Younger, they idealized their future and now, it is their present and it contains nothing they planned for: no corporate lawyer, no dentist, no renowned writer… their love life is a Saharan desert, they, therefore, have to fake happiness since they can't be truly happy.

"Very well." Her emotional state does not really make me sad but her dental braces bother me considerably.

"Really?!"

"You'll see Marie for the details. "

My eyes wickedly sparkle, a redhead will do the trick.

"I don't know how to thank you! "

"Start by getting out of my way."

"Of course, sorry!"

She finally opens this damn door and I quickly walk down the long hallway that leads to my desk, strongly hoping that my New York correspondent has not hung up. It could be an unprecedented business opportunity and I am not the kind of person to ignore opportunities when they come to me.

CHAPTER 3

Monday, May 1st, 10:30 a.m.

I comfortably sit down in my executive armchair and I proudly take this mysterious call with the idea that my prestigious reputation now spreads over the borders.

"Hello?"

"Baroness?"

"Who am I speaking to?"

"My name is Jennifer Adams." A thirty-something, by the sound of her voice. "I'd like to meet you urgently."

"What for?"

"I need your services." I should have guessed it was a client. They're the only ones to hold on the line for so long. "Could we meet in New York?"

"I'm sorry, I don't travel abroad for business."

"I really need your help."

She sounds worried.

"What's so urgent?"

"I can't talk on the phone."

It is certainly an intimidation case: a bit too invasive ex, a violent husband... Many women find themselves terrified to speak.

"Rest assured, you are on a secure line."

I hear her breathing into the receiver.

"No line is secure enough."

"Is this a bad joke?"

It doesn't sound like one.

"I'm sorry to have bothered you."

"Hello?"

She hung up.

I put the phone down.

The emergency will probably push her to call back. They always do.

CHAPTER 4

Monday, May 1st, 12:15 a.m.

I often have lunch at *Fouquet's*, a historic restaurant located at the corner of the Champs-Elysées and Avenue George V. It is one of the best addresses in the capital and the Paris smart set regularly meets there between two business appointments. After having waved to over a dozen people, I promptly go to the table where my friend Chloe, one of the most prominent tax advisors of Paris, is seated. Chloe manages the fortune of wealthy men and she monthly provides me with accounting files of all tax evaders. I use them to put pressure on all high society cheating husbands and my clients adore it.

"You're late, B...."

"Not at all, I always arrive fifteen minutes after everyone else, it's a very subtle way of maintaining people's interest."

I take off my trench coat and sink gracefully on the black velvet bench.

"A few more minutes and I was leaving with this."

She points the holy grail, soberly laid on the table. My amused gaze gets lost in this stack of files that gathers fraudulent financial data of a whole bunch of unfaithful husbands: hidden assets, offshore accounts, dummy companies, in short, all that could destroy a wealthy man.

"I shudder with pleasure."

"I too, exult, when you destroy a man's life."

Chloe duly hates all men.

"That's the reason why you ordered that bottle of champagne, you're celebrating their descent to hell?"

"No, the *Dom P.* is for you."

"You know I don't drink."

It so fiercely alters cognitive functions.

"You'll probably make an exception today," she says, a hint of a smile playing on her lips.

"What should I celebrate?"

"Your first offshore account."

She hands me a black leather pouch. I delicately open it, it contains official documents of a Nassau bank.

"I've never seen anything so beautiful."

"Your clients' romantic setbacks clearly make you happy."

"Three million in the Bahamas, to me, that's an orgasm."

"Then let's try to celebrate this properly."

A waiter interrupts us.

"Ladies, may I take your order?"

"One moment, please." I put the pouch and the accounting files on the bench seat, and I grab the menu in the search of the costliest dish. "The royal lobsters, please. Chloe?"

"I'll have the duck *foie gras* from the Landes"

"Perfect, I'll bring that to you at once."

He goes away but rejoicing keeps coming. I too, lay a present on the table: an envelope full of cash.

"Day of celebration for you as well."

Chloe gets a monthly five percent commission on my fees.

"Not this month, no."

"Why not?"

"Thanks to you, I've already achieved my best financial year," she confesses, drunk with joy.

"How is that possible?"

"You're panicking the city, B., all married men want to put their money in safety, it's unforeseen."

What a cruel conspiracy. These unfaithful husbands think they're putting their money in safety with a renowned tax advisor, who is none other than the treacherous best friend of the woman who will destroy them.

"I impress myself."

No, I'm swelling with self-satisfaction.

"You can, you allow me to triple my income."

"Well, I'm glad to see your business is doing as well as mine."

"As long as you'll manage the love life of all the cheated wives in Paris sixteen, I'll have nothing to worry about."

"Then you owe me."

"Absolutely, and lunch is on me."

"Ladies, here are your royal lobsters in a core of sour fennel ceviche and your duck *foie gras* from the Landes, poached and roasted in a fig leaf. Enjoy your meal."

We look at our courses with relish.

The starred chef always concocts fascinating culinary treasures, they are as good for the palate as they are for the ego.

"By the way, how was your appointment at Rothschild?"

"It's scheduled for next week."

Opening an account in that rich people's bank will undeniably mark my entry among the greats of this world.

"How do you feel about it?"

"It should go just fine." As always, incidentally. I succeeded to climb all the steps of the social ladder and no obstacle ever stopped me.

"Your investments are lucrative, your fortune is increasing…" It's not over yet, I'm aiming at the top. "You'll be a billionaire someday."

I know.

"The question is: how many more frightened virgins will I have to put up with before then?"

Oh, so important existential question between two bites of lobster.

"How many did you see this month?"

"One hundred and twenty, of which nineteen dental braces," I say ironically, while scanning their distress e-mails on my smartphone.

"Do the dental braces shoot up with Xanax?"

"All of my clients shoot up with Xanax."

Lunches with Chloe always hold a little mocking. Although I'm subject to confidentiality clauses, I can't help mentioning the ludicrous situations I daily witness.

"Do you still receive bras by mail?"

What to say about those who can't find Mr. Right and inevitably end up falling into lesbianism?

"We donate those to charities."

"Gosh, I love your job!"

She giggles.

"Would you still love it if I told you that my clients pay me visits at three a.m.?"

"As long as they pay for your shopping sprees…"

I lean the head.

"Seen that way, you're not wrong.

"Doesn't that deserve a toast?"

"I'll grant you that, do the honors."

She grabs the bottle of champagne from the Ice bucket in

which it magnificently placed, skillfully uncorks it, and fills our glasses.

"To the rim?"

"Obviously."

We raise our glasses.

"To your very first offshore account, to your appointment at Rothschild, and to all your cheated Paris sixteenth wives!"

"To all those other clients getting high on Xanax who pay my shopping sprees!"

"Cheers!"

We continue our lunch in opulence and gibes until I notice the time.

"I'm late!"

I stand up in a hurry and put on my trench coat.

"Where are you going?"

"I have to put a tail on an unfaithful husband."

"Finish your meal at least!"

"I don't have time, enjoy for the both of us until our next lunch."

"You didn't tell when!"

"Have your assistant call mine to schedule it!"

I rush out of the restaurant with my bag in my right hand and my arms full of files.

CHAPTER 5

Monday, May 1st, 2:00 p.m.

At the office, I have an immense dressing room which contains tailor-made dress suits and less sophisticated outfits I use for tails. I won't necessarily need that today, but I have thirty minutes to prepare my surveillance equipment. My job leaves very little room for inaction and the fact of having a sports car that can reach two hundred kilometers in less than ten seconds often make me feel like a superheroine in service to women. I admit that the feeling is not unpleasant. And let's be honest, I like to hunt down men and punish them for their wrongdoings. Those whose lives I infiltrate always have things to hide. Some of them are faithful fans of adult websites, others would rather cast a glance and fantasize, and there are those who devilishly act out.

Today's target is a wealthy businessman I've been chasing for months. After having tapped his phone and installed spyware on his computer, I discovered he owns a house in Switzerland, with his large-breasted mistress. Today, they celebrate their affair's first anniversary and she flies from Zürich on a private jet he specially chartered for the occasion. I, therefore, have very little time to install my cameras in the suite they booked. Our lovebirds have chosen to settle in one of the most luxurious hotels in Paris, close to the very chic Place Vendôme. The suite is a nice size, the bathroom is marble, the chandeliers are in crystal, and a vintage bottle of champagne has been carefully placed on the lounge area. Many details that foster the feeling of absolute power among wealthy husbands. At least, until I enter their lives to set them straight.

I installed cameras in false smoke detectors and I positioned them high up in every part of the suite. My clients only believe what they see. I always provide them with their husbands' sex tapes. It clearly stimulates their desire for revenge and I care about that. Men who betray their wives must be punished, that's my rule. My clients know it and when they come to me, they buy back their dignity, incidentally. Thanks to me, they're no longer submissive wives that adultery crossed out with shame, they are the ones who punish and whose husbands implore forgiveness on their knees.

"Thanks, B.!"

"Thank you, Julie."

Julie is one of the hotel's chambermaids. I grease everybody's palms here. The staff is underpaid and they see nothing wrong with earning some extra cash to help make ends meet. Receptionists give me the suite numbers, chambermaids open them, and security officers erase me off the video recordings. I use this exchange process in every starred hotel in Paris. Hotel establishments are places to favor when you want to unveil infidelity. Illicit couples don't show themselves in public, they prefer closed and discreet areas. My target is no exception from the rule and will definitely spend the day here. He planned a spa cares and a gourmet dinner on the terrace, with a view overlooking the Paris rooftops. What a pity he hasn't been as romantic with his own wife, because tomorrow the case will be closed and I'll see him at the office to set things straight.

CHAPTER 6

Monday, May 1st, 3:00 p.m.

My two next clients shouldn't be long. I gave them an appointment at a café and I'm waiting for them on the terrace with a good cup of green tea. In spring, it's not rare to see me strike a pose with my Ray-Ban Aviator, on terraces of the trendiest cafés in Paris. I had the common sense of creating a job that allows me to mix business with pleasure and enjoying a moment of relaxation in the middle of the afternoon is a luxury I give myself quite often.

"Miss?" I raised the head. What is this atrocious thing so violently entering my intimate space, hands casually placed in pockets, and hips rudely thrust forwards? "I'm sorry to bother you, I was seating two tables from you and couldn't help but noticing how…"

Hot I am?

"I know."

He's not the only one to go into raptures.

"May I offer you a drink?"

"It's useless, you're wasting your time."

I don't like square-toe shoes, cheap suits, bad breaths, and let alone face molds.

"Dinner, lunch?"

Even being charitable, he wouldn't stand a minute with a woman like me.

"You should leave."

If he doesn't want a Taser shot.

"Very well, have a good day anyway!"

"Good luck to you!"

He's not going anywhere without getting rid of the repulsion he inspires to women. Men's vision of relationships is so narrow. Systematically thinking their male status will enable them to get all the women they want. I often bring them back to the 21st century's reality.

CHAPTER 7

Monday, May 1st, 4:00 p.m.

"Hello, B?"

"Sophie!" My field assistant.

"Am I disturbing you?"

"No, I'm waiting for my clients in a café."

"I have some news about young Aurelie's case."

"Tell me."

"I paid David a small visit along with Yuri." Yuri is a Cerberus I use to intimidate the targets. It's not very conventional but it is nonetheless very effective. "I confirm that he won't come within a hundred meters from her."

"And for the art history classes?"

"He won't set foot there again."

"It's obvious that he was just there to shop around."

"Hello, Baroness."

"Sophie, I'm leaving you, my client has just arrived."

I hang up.

"I'm sorry, I didn't want to interrupt."

She says, after doing it…

"Please Claire, sit." Claire is a young dynamic executive, graduated with a master in communication, who ironically doesn't know how to communicate.

"Would you like a tea, a coffee?"

"Oh no, thanks. I couldn't possibly swallow anything."

She's way too eager to see the phishing plan I concocted for her.

"Here's what we talked about." I hand her twelve Word pages outlining how she could corner her work colleague. They have often made visual contact but never talked to each other. The target plays shy and must therefore be discreetly driven into our nets. "As you know, feminine seduction is a passive process. We never approach men directly but always by devious means. I made you a list, but we'll only use the most effective way which is asking them for help." Her curiosity seems to get lost in the pages, she shouldn't be hasty. "Stay on page two, Claire, it's important to go through the details of the plan together so that it's…" Clear?

"Of course, sorry! I'm just a little nervous about the part I'll have to play."

The part of a grounded and well-adjusted woman.

"Tomorrow morning, you'll go to your company's archives room to get files. Make sure they're bulky enough to form a stack you will have trouble to carry. You'll leave them in your office until 3:58 p.m., our target will get out of his at 4 p.m., you'll have two minutes to join him. Once you do, you'll clumsily drop them."

"It looks rather easy," she says, puzzled.

I grinned maliciously, she'll soon become disillusioned.

"Actually, in practice, it's more complicated. I insist on the fact that you shouldn't drop the files if he's accompanied, on the phone, in a hurry, has his head bent down or is staring into space. For the phishing to succeed, the target's body and mind have to be fully available"

"What if he doesn't help me?"

"He will." Men love to make themselves useful to (pretty) women. "You'll then have six minutes and thirty-nine seconds to reach the archives room. It's, in other words, the time that you'll be given for a conversation."

"What should we talk about?"

"You're overworked." Hence the stack of files. "You work too much, you need a break, which will end up in a date offer."

"Wait, I'm not ready for a date," she objects, nervously.

Single thirty-something women are as emotional as twenty years old girls.

"He won't invite you that day." It's all very young, it'll take an extra week before he does. "He'll first want to make sure you share his feelings."

"And that he likes me?"

"He does." The way he looks at her largely witness for his interest. "And he'll like you even more tomorrow." Circumstances will devilishly be set for that to happen. "The archives room will be empty, lights will be dim, the atmosphere will be intimate and conducive to mind's well-being. This will increase your emotional sensitivity for both of you."

I frown, why do I hear her heart beat the drums?

"You're stressing me out…"

"Do you want a Xanax?"

"No, thank you. I've quit."

She obviously shouldn't have. Her forehead is dripping and her arms are as stiff as poles.

"Relax Claire, there's no reason for you to worry."

"I was far from thinking it would be a date."

"It's nothing more than a first approach. The staging might seem frightening but it only aims at easing the phishing phase."

We'll have to get her married someday.

"What if I can't make it?"

"Follow the plan and everything will go fine."

"What if he kisses me, if he jumps at me?"

If he gives her what she wants?

"That won't happen." We are not on a TV show. "Men aren't so confident. You'll have a small talk and each of you will go back to minding their errands."

"It's much better." She finally slows down her breathing. "What'll happen next?"

"We'll head over to the coffee machine to strengthen your bond." Page six – condition the target's brain by accustoming it to the client's visual presence in accordance with Ivan Pavlov's conditioning method. "He's there every day at 4:03 p.m., you'll get there at 4:00 p.m., more and more smiling as days go by. My assistant Sophie will make you up every morning to gradually increase the desire." We'll use contouring to symmetries each part of her face, based on the golden ratio, a proportion used by ancient Greeks as a measure of physical perfection.

"I'd rather have him see me natural."

Then, let her start by coming out from the ton of foundation beneath which she's already buried.

"You'll recover your beauty routine when he's completely overwhelmed."

"If he only had sex in mind, these makeup sessions wouldn't help. I don't want that."

When clients foolishly think they can teach you your job.

"Claire, the target just signed on a mortgage for a house. He does home improvements most of his free time and he only goes out every two weekends. Moreover, his eyes aren't focusing on your body but on your face. His signs are very clear, he's not looking for a one-night woman but for the one of his life."

"What if he came to understand that I'm not that woman, because too superficial?"

"The ten daily minutes you'll spend together at the coffee machine will give him plenty of time to notice your kindness, your spirit, your intellect…" Her crooked nose, her squint. "… and your long golden hair that'll give him wonderful little blond children." Clients pay the bills, so I need to flatter them from time to time. "Take my word for it, you're widely good for each other. I'm just getting your foot on the ladder."

She'll thank me after an unwanted pregnancy and an early wedding.

"What if he doesn't invite me despite all those positive points?"

Women's brain is a dust factory that constantly needs to be vacuumed. Luckily, I'm not concerned, I'm gifted.

"My plan has been developed to allow you to reach your goals but it's not excluded that the target takes a bit more time than necessary to invite you. In such a case, I absolutely forbid you to make the first move." Crazy ideas sometimes get into their heads. "You'll never ask him out, you won't call him, and you won't immediately answer his calls either."

She shrugs.

"I'm way too shy for that."

Like all of them, before and after her.

"Your inhibitions will soon fade away and make room for unwavering confidence." She'll end up feeling so comfortable with him, that she'll do whatever it takes to have him in her life. "I'm drawing your attention to the fact that you'll absolutely have to control yourself."

"You'll be there to chaperone me?"

"Sophie will handle that." She takes over all the dirty work I want to get rid of. "She'll whisper you the answers at the coffee machine." Among other unfortunate chores which make you want to question your whole existence and incidentally, stab yourself.

"And as for the date?"

"I won't be able to attend either."

I'll have other things to do. I don't know what yet, but they'll certainly be more interesting than a morose and shy conversation between two terrified thirty-something.

"So I won't see you again?"

"Unfortunately…" For her. "No, but you'll always be welcome at the office."

"Really?"

"Of course!"

As long as she pays for it!

CHAPTER 8

Monday, May 1st, 5:00 p.m.

"Waiter, two sugared green teas, please."

I'm coming close to hypoglycemia. Facing all those nuts clients is no small feat. Each of them comes with its share of eccentricities and craziness, and I always end up, despite of myself, impersonating a therapist. Here comes one of them, desperately trying to make her way between the café's tables with her crossbody discount bag, the end of the day promises to be very fun.

"Baroness, here you are!"

"Do I really have a choice?"

She doesn't notice my cynicism. Too bad, she sits.

"I'm so relieved to see you! After what happened this morning, I thought you wouldn't come." I shouldn't have. "Here, I brought you a surprise." How unfortunate, she gives me a heart-shaped box. "Those are peppermint cookies encrusted with carob seeds."

Why do clients always insist on giving me presents that are all more fanciful than the other? Emoji mugs, anti-stress balls, aroma diffusers, giant sombreros... I'm entitled to all that provokes repulsion.

"How very thoughtful."

I place it on the table until I can discreetly toss it in the trash can.

"That's not all! Here's a mini-office-vacuum cleaner if you want to savor them between two appointments!"

That will join the broom closet, where we store all the clients' outlandish gifts. Marie often goes there to help herself whenever she's having a yard sale.

"You shouldn't have."

"It's three times nothing, really." Indeed, it's three times nothing. "You've been so understanding this morning!" I have no recollection of that. "Was my reaction excessive?"

"No, that was a classic reaction." Of a frightened virgin. "How do you feel?"

"Better." The Xanax had an effect. "Has David arrived? I haven't found him."

She looks around her. Useless to look for him, he will never come.

The waiter sets down the cups of tea.

"Drink while waiting for him."

"And to think that we're talking about the university's soccer team captain!" All I've seen is a bodybuilder kid with a head in the form of testicles, which says a lot about clients idealizing their beloved one. "Did you pay him to come?"

"No, those are not my work methods."

"I'm sure you paid him!" I sip my tea; I really need a significant dose of energy to end the day. "What kind of guy would date me without being paid?" Probably none. "I'm too pale, too skinny, too shy…" And mostly too tortured.

"Aurelie, David cares about you."

Her eyes open wide.

"Really?!"

"He does but not the way you think…" Let's not rejoice

too fast. "… because he's a compulsive collector who likes all women."

That womanizer is like all the other ones chasing their prey on campuses. All of them emerge from this painful acne period imposed by puberty and their entry into the adult world turns out to be a liberation, which allows them to realize all their fantasies.

"I know he likes women, fortunately, otherwise I would have reasons to worry."

"Only to him, they're just pleasure tools he uses to content his own desires. He can't offer a healthy relationship since he's mentally disturbed."

"I'm not following."

"David suffered from anorexia when he was younger. His self-image has long been an issue, then he forged himself a body stuffed with creatine. Now, he's making up for lost times. He plays with words, charm, anything that will get him the girls he wants. In other words, he's not your target, you're his."

An ideal target for all Freddy Kruegers in search of fresh meat food.

"How do you know all that?"

"I consulted his academic medical records." On the famous Sorbonne University database. The IT department should really improve its firewalls.

"So, you're telling me that the only guy I ever liked is actually a psycho?"

Does it seem that surprising?

"I'm afraid so."

Her eyes wander about.

"What's wrong with me?"

I am inclined to say everything, but…

"I'll let you interpret the situation."

"So what now, will I have to hug the walls?"

"He's not violent, just addicted to sex."

Which is enough of petrifying flaw to repel any decent woman.

"What if I like it?"

"I beg your pardon?"

"What if I want to have fun?"

This joyful reaction is unexpected, to say the least.

"I doubt it's a smart idea."

But it is a choice.

"I mean really, I've spent seventeen years of my life trying to please my parents. I went to music academy for them, I majored in literature for them, I passed all my exams, and I feel like I haven't lived!" she says while madly gesticulating. Why should I care? "What if I wanted to experiment that?" More power to you!

"If you go out with David, you won't be able to dump him so easily. You're young, and you're not very experienced, so you'll firmly hang on to him."

Like all the virgins her age.

"Too late, you said yourself, I'm in love with him! Remember this morning in your office?"

About that, I'm wondering where the docile groupie went?

"You're not at the physical experimentation stage yet, you're daydreaming. If you stop everything now, it will have minimal impact. You'll be sad for a few days, but you'll feel better very quickly. However, if you experience physical contact, it will destroy you."

"So what do we do now?"

I blame her insolence on the emotional shock.

"I'll give you a choice."

"If I want to go to the date?"

"I'll set you up with a listening device including an earpiece and a microphone connected to mine so that we can discreetly communicate."

"What other solution is there? Spend my entire life under my parent's yoke?"

"You protect yourself and wait for a man who will make you truly happy. Which is to me the continuity of a life you've brilliantly mastered until now."

She takes ownership of endless thinking seconds that should not take long to make me dizzy.

"Damn, I paid for a guy who I finally won't get?" And who turns out to be mentally ill. "I'm even wearing my best clothes for him!" Which is an ugly white blouse with black polka dots, hideously matched with horrendous plastic ballet flats. "I'm so angry with myself!"

Bitterness and disappointment always inevitably conclude the romantic dreams of these slightly too hurried virgins.

"You shouldn't, you're a young woman promised to a brilliant future. You just need to learn not to invest so much for a man unless he's your spouse. That's your first life lesson."

"How did I get fooled?"

"You've let emotions take over reason and let yourself get tricked by all his compliments. In other words, you idealized him." That's typical of Ugly Bettys.

"I love you so much!"

"As you should, now it's time to make a decision." It's always wiser to let clients believe they decide what the turn of events will be. "David just got here, do you want to join him?"

Her frown says a lot.

"I won't give him satisfaction!"

"That's a wise decision." I'll be able to shorten this

appointment and go for a massage. "Now…" I take a file and a pen out of my briefcase. "… sign this."

She takes it.

"What is it?"

"A supplemental agreement to our contract certifying that you've been informed of David's medical history, of his current health state, and of the risk that you incur if you go against my recommendations. The second page is a consent form which enables us to close the initial contract that you signed this morning."

My fortune matters far too much to me to let it go crumbling away in the courts.

"I'm lost… you're such a pro!"

Her signature marks the official closing of her file, which by the way, I carefully put away in my bag and since all charity has its limits…

"Aurelie, I wish you a good rest of the day."

And good luck for the next steps of her life.

"That's all?"

She looks surprised.

"What else did you expect?"

"I don't know…" She pulls a face while scratching the 22-inch screen she has instead of a forehead. "That was really short."

I stand up.

"I've done my job, now I go on with my life and you should do likewise."

I put my bag on my shoulder and I quickly head toward my car without giving her the time to react, valedictions have never been my strength.

"Baroness, wait!" I knew it! I'm always get grabbed a few meters further! "Wait!" I turn around. "You forgot your gifts!"

And I thought I subtly got rid of those.

"You literally saved my life."

She tucks them in my arms, how in the hell can I thank her?

"We could have one last drink together…" I raise my eyebrows in surprise, have I just heard that? "It would be a good idea…"

"No, it's not going to happen. Have a good day Aurelie."

I keep walking. She follows me.

"Why not?"

What a dreamer!

"Aurelie, the party is over, everyone goes home now."

"And tomorrow, or the day after tomorrow?" Subway is two steps away, I often think of throwing myself under a train. "I could give you my number and you'll call me when…"

"Here we go!" Harassment, intrusions, hangdog look, blues… "That's why I dread so much the moment of separations when I handle a pro bono!"

" A pro bono?"

"Yes, you're a pro bono, my good deed of the month. That's the reason why I accepted your case. Don't give me any regrets!"

"A pro bono at five hundred euros an hour?"

"I usually don't do teenagers and students."

"So why did you receive me?"

"Out of soul kindness, that's all!"

"None of it was serious?"

"Of course, it was! I treated like any other client and I gave you all the professionalism that you were entitled to expect, but don't think that a woman like me would enjoy infiltrating the life of a seventeen-year-old kid!"

"What does it mean?"

"That I have no intention of having a drink with you, that

I don't want your phone number, and even less take selfies. I'd just like to leave without it being a source of conflict!"

"What if I need your services?"

"Then call my assistant and make an appointment! Just don't forget, I charge five hundred euros an hour and there's usually a 6-month waiting list!"

I enter my car, start the ignition, and madly press down on the accelerator, ditching her there as if I was insensitive and never had been seventeen myself. I know well, like all of them, she doesn't want me to leave. My presence reassures them. They lack bearings and I'm the only one able to provide them some. I'm therefore a bit like their mentor and they all dream of joining my social circle. I always call them back to order because it is very important to set limits with clients. Especially with students who are subject to emotional intoxication. That's also why I limit their visits to the office. I only see them once a month, and it's more than enough for me. The rest of the time is dedicated to more forewarned clients whose purchasing power far exceeds that of ordinary people. That way, everyone finds their niche and me mostly.

CHAPTER 9

Monday, May 1st, 6:30 p.m.

I enter the spa. Two hostesses quickly welcome me. The first one takes my personal belongings, the second one leads me to the dressing room. I undress and put on a swimming suit for the jacuzzi, prelude of a long moment of relaxation I wouldn't trade for a fortune. In this wellness oasis, my thoughts wander, my mind regenerates, and the massage bubbles which caress my skin in time with the background music, take me on a sensory journey revealing joys and wonders. I instantly forget the daily frenzy, so heavily marked by the immense hope all those damned clients have set on me. Here, my responsibilities vanish just like sweat in the sauna. I class complaints into folders of disregard and lamentations no longer have the slightest ounce of hearing within these walls of bliss. Here, I am someplace else, in a world which is entirely different from the one of all these tortured women, whose lives daily drown in chaos, and the memory of them doesn't surpass the one of the substantial income their tribulations so generously provide to my personal comfort.

After the jacuzzi, the sauna, and the essential oils massage, I savor this outpouring enjoyment near a 50-foot long swimming pool. Its bottom is covered with an Italian mosaic of white and blue oriental patterns, and side columns esthetically separate it from the deck chair on which I'm laying. There is a cup of Matcha on the side table. It has been served with a few chocolates, a fashion magazine, and my smartphone is close at hand. My private inbox is full of positive messages that will help revitalize me and I always choose this moment to read them. I find countless love worlds from my beloved one, Chloe's cheerful camaraderie, invitations to high society events, and many other requests and sycophancies, which contribute so much to make me what I am and will remain: a woman who so ardently wallows in navel-gazing and who wouldn't want to change for anything in the world.

CHAPTER 10

Tuesday, May 2nd, 9:00 a.m.

"Good morning, Baroness!"

"Good morning, Marie."

"Here's your orange juice, your messages, and your schedule for the day."

"I'm listening, Marie."

"The Von Beck Gala's organizer wants to confirm your presence this evening, you're closing case *#4952* at 3:00 p.m., you're seeing the client at 11:00 a.m. and the target is already in your office."

Perfect, we're going to clear things up. The closing of an infidelity case necessarily involves confronting the target. The stakes are such that my clients let me handle this negotiation which, for the sake of domination, always take place at my office. The address is prestigious, the furniture is luxurious, and the floor-to-ceiling windows offer a breathtaking view of the city's highest buildings. Enough to set the tone to our guests and clearly highlight the supremacy of the one defending their wives 'interests.

"Good morning, Mr. Meyer."

Jacques Meyer, yesterday's unfaithful husband. He's

enjoying his coffee with such innocence, no one could guess he's been under the radar for so long.

"Good morning, I've received a summons."

He hands it to me.

"Not anymore."

I put it in the paper shredder to make all traces of our meeting disappear.

"What is this about?"

"Personal matters. Yours," I say dryly while opening file *#4952.*

"My understanding was that my tax situation requires some clarifications. Are you a Treasury Department Agent?"

He's as stupid as he's ugly. As brilliant as I am, I still can't understand why women marry their antithesis.

"Haven't you seen the plate at the office entrance?"

I deliberately avoid any visual contact to show him my contempt.

"It's written B Consulting."

"Indeed, I'm a consultant, not a tax inspector."

"Thank you but I don't need any tax advice."

He stands up, a bit too confident.

"Sit!"

"I beg your pardon?"

I raise my head and transfix him with my disdainful gaze.

"You heard me, sit down immediately!"

Yuri gets in the office. He closes the door, blocks it with his corpulence, and firmly crosses his arms.

"What does that mean?"

"Yuri is my bodyguard, he is Serbian, he's over 6 and a half feet tall, and as you can see, he has a quite impressive muscular mass."

He could cut off his toes with a pair of pliers and pull out his teeth with no anesthesia.

"What's that? Mafia extortion?"

It's more like sequestration.

"Actually, I've been hired by your wife to assert your misconduct."

He sits back down with inquiring eyes.

I take this opportunity to give him a file of pictures in which he will certainly recognize his micro-penis.

"Are you a private investigator?"

"Not really."

I have never been able to define my job. Let's say that there is, on one hand, the respectable consultant who goes around high society events, and on the other hand, the seduction expert who often flirts with illegality.

"What do you want?"

"Compensation for my client."

"Let her file for divorce."

"You didn't understand me."

"It's all very clear."

"I summoned you to rip you off, not to negotiate. "

"You'll need more than a bunch of photos to make me bend over."

He fakes self-control but I'm not fooled. Unfaithful husbands spend colossal amounts of time developing plans to avoid getting caught and the idea of being found-out makes them constantly nervous. As soon as I entered the office, I had plenty of time to intoxicate myself with the anguish his body surreptitiously spreads at every corner of the room.

"Marie, bring me a cup of tea with a drop of milk, please."

We're going to take this a step further.

"Yes, Baroness."

I toss him another file which he hurriedly opens with frightened eyes.

"It compiles all of your tax scams, including your offshore accounts: Belize, Delaware, Cayman Islands, Tel-Aviv, Hong Kong… Your tax lawyer's financial schemes are very ingenious and the Dutch sandwich is particularly brilliant."

Chloe is obviously one of the most brilliant women I know.

"How did you get these documents?!"

Here he is dumbfounded. In a few seconds, he'll probably pee in his pants.

"Legally speaking, this has very little importance. However, tax evasion is subject to a three million-euro fine and seven years in prison. The cell in which you'll sleep will have nothing in common with one of a luxury hotel, but Yuri's friends will welcome you adequately."

"But who are you, for GOD's sake?!"

"I'm the one who destroys men with unbridled virility."

I have no compassion for these jerks. To me, they're just simple appetizers to be eaten, one after the other.

"I'm not the kind of man that you think."

"A womanizer who wasn't able to hold back the tiny worm he uses for a penis?"

"I never wanted to hurt my wife."

"And yet, you destroyed her."

His wife hasn't been informed yet but the assertion is a very efficient manipulation method to increase guilt.

"It's her fault! She always gives me the feeling of being useless and powerless, I'm never good enough to her!" he shouts in a whirlwind of gestures.

"I don't care about your soul-searching."

Neither do I care about his sudden pitiful glances.

"I just needed some affection." Big pig. "I just needed to exist as a man."

"You're far from being one! A real man carries his wife in each challenge their marriage goes through!"

"I tried!"

"By dipping your biscuit in another woman's butt?"

"It doesn't change anything to my love for her!"

Dirty liar.

"It's going to change a lot of things about your bank account."

The more men cheat, the more they have to pay. I always convert their adulterous bedtime frolics into a lump sum. It doesn't entirely make up for the heartaches, but it is a significant financial compensation which allows my clients to start over again.

"Do you really think I'll give my money that easily?"

"Would you rather go to jail?"

"I have very good lawyers."

And I have a very good network.

"You'll be brought up for immediate trial. The people who'll handle your case are women who also have been betrayed by their husbands. We all are feminists, which implies a profound love for our sisters and a limitless willingness to destroy any man who'd hurt them."

"I want to speak to my wife."

He takes his phone.

"That's useless."

We always require our clients to turn theirs off during confrontations.

"Where is she?"

Not very far away, in the boardroom.

"It's over, you won't ever see her again."

"That's insane," he says with a forced laugh.

"You misbehaved and now you'll disappear."

"We'll see about that."

Yuri tightens his jaw even before he has time to stand up.

"Needless to say, you'd risk fatal consequences if you ever dared to attempt reconciliation."

"You have no right standing between us!"

"I'm defending your wife's interests. Legally speaking, I'm entitled to anything."

"I've had enough!"

"If this meeting seems endless to you, think about the long painful hours you'd have to endure behind bars."

"All this is just a farce!"

"Do you really want to bet your whole life on this delusional hope?" I say boastfully with an impassive face.

"Let me go!"

"I'm the one setting rules here and the best advice I can give you is to undo your tie because the following minutes will be the most intense moment of your entire existence."

And for a reason: men relieved from their wealth are just like men sodomized without any lubricant.

"I'm calling my lawyer."

"Your lawyer quit twenty-six minutes and thirty-seven seconds ago."

A tea with a drop of milk… that's the sign that allows Marie to call our allies.

"Jacques Meyer for Laura Simon."

Laura Simon is none other than my golf partner.

"You'll end up realizing that you have no way out."

He hangs up, stunned. The office secretary probably sent him packing.

"Why?" To weaken his most profound convictions.

"Times have changed, Jacques. These days, women own the world and none of them will agree to defend the cause of a white-collar criminal who jumps on anything that moves."

"How much do you expect to get from me, a million?

"Is that all the freedom of a man your standing is worth?"

A man who enjoys life without moderation has everything to lose by ending it.

"I'm ready to pay two million if you give me all copies of those files."

"Don't be fooled by my sex-appeal, Jacques, I'm far from being a amateur."

"I'll give you five."

"I want sixty percent of your personal fortune in my client's bank account."

I hand him a file.

"What is it?"

"A contract."

"I haven't agreed yet."

"You should hurry."

After all, who can boast about being able to pay for their years of prison?

"I want to read it first."

"Marie, bring Mr. Meyer the digital tablet."

"Wait a minute! Clause number two, the husband undertakes to give the marital home to his wife?!"

"You'll no longer step foot there."

"No way, I'm keeping the house!"

"Are domestic quarrels and lies the kind of memory that you cherish?"

"I have my reasons."

"Unfortunately, none of this contract's clause is up for discussion."

"That's unbelievable!"

I admit it's a high price to pay for hanky-panky.

"In the future, you'll think twice before lowering your pants in front of strangers."

Marie enters and hands him the tablet.

"What should I do with this?"

"Sign the contract and make your transfer, bank details are on it."

"What about the files?"

"They'll remain temporarily in my possession."

I want to make sure that this die-hard cheater doesn't breach his contractual obligations.

"When will I be able to have them back?"

"You'll be kept informed."

"I need a date."

"Make do with a promise."

I hold his gaze until he ends up fulfilling as instructed.

"It's done."

I take the tablet back.

"Congratulations, you can leave the premises You'll be free in 48 hours."

"I don't understand…"

"Yuri will remain in your company until the funds are fully available."

"Is that really necessary?"

"Undeniably."

Women of power enjoy enslaving men. Seeing him walk out the door, after crushing him with my domination, makes me come as much as copulation. Since the orgasm is over, he's now dismissed.

CHAPTER 11

Tuesday, May 2nd, 10:00 a.m.

Now, off to the boardroom where all discreditable secrets of the Parisian elite pile up: mistresses, premium call girls, sadomasochistic penchant, bi, and homosexuality. The double lives that husbands try so hard to hide and that always end up revealing to their wife.

"Good morning, Camille."

Camille Meyer, a distinguished wife whose life is about to tumble.

"Good morning," she says with a distraught face, staring blankly, the hollow eyes.

Nothing surprising, cheated wives we summon to the office are so obsessed by the conclusion of the investigation that they can't sleep at night.

"Marie, bring a cup of ginseng to Mrs. Meyer, please."

"No, thank you."

"I insist."

The nervous tics resulting from that insomnia will soon end up annoying me.

"I just want to know where we stand and end this as soon as possible."

We're getting there.

"Let me first resume the points we've talked about during our first appointment." I solemnly open file *#4952*. "It was about unveiling your husband's true life which, according to your statements, had nothing in keeping with the one he officially showed, and thus…"

"Blah-blah-blah…"

What?!

"What did you say ?!

"You don't have to list all the reasons why I hired you! I'm aware, I was there!" Maybe I should give her the intravenous injection of Xanax we save for our untamable clients!"Just tell me if my husband is cheating on me!"

"Every week for the last year!" I'm not rejoicing to break such news, in such a rushed way, but let's admit she had it coming. "Three-quarters of his business trips are only smoke-screens to let him meet his mistress." I willingly ram home the news and she suddenly no longer shows any apparent emotion.

Let's note that separations are experienced like periods of mourning. They're less painful but they include more or less similar phases. This impassive face reveals the first phase of the process: the shock.

"Do you have proof of what you're saying?" she asks with frightened eyes.

"Obviously." E-mail exchanges, audio recordings, high-definition pictures, 3D videos…"Here." A picture.

"Two adults holding hands?" Let's go crescendo to avoid a heart attack. "Is that all you got?"

"Here's another one."

It portrays two particularly demonstrative adults touching their genitals. Hard to deny the facts.

"I don't see very well…"

Phase two: denial. Tribute to all those refusing to admit the man of their life is a bastard.

"Marie, bring the video projector, please."

We're going to take this a step further.

"Yes, Baroness."

"Are you sure this is my husband?"

"Camille, I investigated your husband for several long months. I intercepted his bank statements, I bugged his phone, I tailed him many times. I can assure I know his life better than he knows it himself."

Knowing he's allergic to macadamia nuts would allow me to kill him without anyone knowing. But rest assured, I don't do crimes, I prefer melodrama, it's much more entertaining.

"You're not answering my question! Are you sure that this is my husband?"

How can you not be cruel to clients who display such a degree of insolence?

"Marie…" She always comes in at the right time. "… glasses!"

She quickly takes them out of their boxes.

"What's that?"

An essential tool that will let her receive the obvious proof that her husband is cheating on her.

"3D glasses."

Marie hands us a pair and saves one for herself. Just like me, Marie loves festivities. She puts the blinds down and switches on the projector. Here we are now, the three of us, in the middle of a porn movie session.

"Should I put on the sound, Baroness?"

"That's not necessary."

Images speak for themselves. I'm incidentally delighted to

have bought that 3D video projector, the testicles coming out of the screen are mammoth!

"OH MY GOD, Jacques!" Her hand on her mouth seems to show a slight feeling of offense. Has she recognized her husband's skin growth? "Filth!" Maybe I should add the sound so she can hear his orgasmic squeaks. "Stop it!" Not yet. "Please, stop the video!" she begs by covering her face with her hands.

"Your husband slept with his mistress four hundred and twelve times." I want to destroy her denial. "Here is a thumb drive that contains the evidence of my claims." I place it at the center of the meeting table. "It includes a whole set of compromising elements and a PowerPoint presentation for more clarity." Enough to keep busy. "Marie, turn off the video projector."

Since the truth has been unveiled, there's no more need to insist.

Marie carries out my instructions and shyly leaves the room.

Our skeptical client slowly uncovers her face wet with tears, I go towards the floor-to-ceiling windows to give her some privacy.

Alone in front of the horizon, I wonder if I locked the garage door this morning. My Porsche features a remote locking system that I probably forgot to activate.

She's sobbing.

I turn around.

"Camille, I know how painful it is."

So many ready-made phrases which we pick up as in a store...

"You know nothing!" So be it. "You hear me? You know nothing!" Phase three: anger. "You've been swaggering around from the very beginning, with your fit model style, and you couldn't care less about me to whom you haven't shown the slightest ounce of empathy!"

"Camille, calm down."

The bawling mixed to the dripping mascara seems eminently frightening to me.

"You break the news that I'm cuckolded and you want me to calm down?" Why doesn't she use the tissues we provided her? "When he proposed in Venice, I cried like a baby. He made my dream come true and now you're wrecking it!"

"I'm not wrecking anything, I'm giving you what you paid for!" Cheated wives quite commonly try to transfer their pig's misconduct on to others, but I refuse to bear the cost! "I'm in no way responsible for your husband's shameful deeds!"

The thoughtful air that suddenly spread over her face disconcerts me.

"Goodness, forgive me, I'm don't know where I stand anymore!" In a clinical bipolar state. "Everything happened so suddenly." Let's pray now that she wipes off her face. "On the other hand, it all seemed so obvious! He was so distracted and aloof! He didn't look at me anymore, he didn't touch me anymore…" No kidding. "We no longer shared anything together!"

"The dwindling of moments of intimacy is one of the most obvious signs of infidelity."

Neglected wives should quickly wonder about the likely existence of a third party within their relationship.

"Who is she?"

"A forty-year-old heading a contemporary art museum in Zürich. Blond, green eyes, average size…" In short, irresistible. "You have nothing to envy her."

"Then, why?"

"Occasions make cheating possible." In addition to

her extremely attractive appearance…"She was there at the right time."

That decisive moment which a lot of married people inevitably go through.

The dissatisfactions accumulate and eventually end up by creating frustrations which must imperatively be satisfied. Within the couple or with a foreign body.

"Is there a tiny chance he's not in love with her?"

"Unfortunately, no. Desire, pleasure, passion… all those special moments his mistress gave him on a silver platter have made him madly in love. They celebrated that yesterday, in a Parisian five stars hotel." Just like in a final *Bachelor* episode. What else can she expect after such a degree of involvement?

"That woman is omnipresent in my husband's life and nevertheless doesn't exist in ours. Why have I never found any trace of lipstick or foundation on his shirt collars, no strand of hair, no fingerprints, no clue, nothing…?"

"Your husband has turned out to be very resourceful during this affair." A true master in the arts of covering tracks. "He always bought two identical shirts, always carried his own shower gel, never kept a receipt, always paid in cash, and he had another cell phone in which his mistress' number was saved under a man's first name." Not to mention the many itineraries changes when he copulated in Paris and the encrypted e-mails that I'm very pleased to have successfully decoded.

"We'd put love locks on the Pont des Arts parapet fence."

This melancholic memory sounds nothing good.

"Marie, have Sophie come to the boardroom, please."

It seems that we've reached stage four, depression.

"I felt a slight heartache when the City Hall took them off, was that a sign?" No, but perhaps it would be good to remind her that stupidly hanging locks on a historical monument is a felony. "Have all couples who vowed their fidelity on this bridge seen their love shatter like me?"

Sophie comes in. Just in time to save me from the usual depressive monologue that cheated wives never skip.

"Camille, let me introduce you to Sophie."

"Hello Sophie, are you married?"

"Stage 4?"

"On the spot. Have a seat." We're going to present the plan which will lead to the cognitive reconstruction of our cheated wife. "Sophie will ensure the follow-up of your file and will supervise you until it is formally closed." Her presence is specially designed to overshadow her husband's and prevent her from doing something irreparable: contact him. That temptation will mostly grow bigger when she thinks about him. It is therefore essential to reorganize her environment. This is the beginning of the withdrawal process. "You'll need to get rid of everything that can remind you of your husband, photos, objects, gifts, jewels, and this, regardless of their financial or emotional value."

"Our mutual friends?"

"And the marital home – genuine Proust's madeleine – that your husband has agreed to give, but that we'll put up for sale, due to the very significant meaning it holds."

"I never thought I would have to leave that house one day… I entered it as a young bride and I thought that I would stay there for the rest of my life." Let's all take out the violins. "I've never considered happiness with any other man except him."

"It's time to raise your expectations."

"I don't want to raise my expectations, I want my husband back."

We exchange a look with Sophie, what hasn't she understood?

"Your husband and his mistress are joint owners of a 300 square meters house in Zürich. Their relationship is nothing but serious and will entail an inexorable divorce." She will never see him again, it's over. "You must prepare yourself psychologically."

"It seems insurmountable," she mutters while staring into space.

"Sophie will be there to help you, she'll assist you for forty days."

Poor her.

"Why forty days?"

"That's the time it takes for your cerebral system to get rid of a habit or integrate a new one." We'll modify the patterns of her consciousness by shifting her onto a new life trajectory. "You'll have a new home, new activities, new itineraries, and by inference, new automatic reflexes."

"Will you handle the divorce as well?"

Sure, anything else?

"Your attorney will."

"I won't have the strength to fight," she sighs listlessly.

"You won't have to. Your husband has consented to several concessions including a large part of his personal fortune. That'll allow you to create the new life we were talking about."

"How can I just brush aside ten years of marriage?"

"Progressively. But if you follow our instructions to the letter, you'll do it much faster than you can imagine."

"How did your previous clients handle it?"

"Brilliantly." Hence my firm's reputation. "Their divorce has turned out to be a fabulous springboard they used to achieve various life goals. You'll do likewise."

"What could I want if my husband isn't by my side?"

"Renaissance, novelty, experience, independence, freedom… You'll go at it without ever feeling that you've had enough." She will make new friends with whom she will attend all sorts of social and cultural events in Paris. She will live a burning love passion with a man she'd never imagined could exist. She will focus on developing an artistic or literary project. She will try a vegan or organic food diet and she will finally take yoga, cooking and salsa classes among other trendsetting activities which never ceased attracting her but which she had to ignore when she got married. "You will get a new lease on life, you'll be full of joy and energy, you'll become more beautiful, more fulfilled, more asserted, and you'll thank me because you will then experience the most beautiful moment of your entire life."

That's the hidden side of separation. Time always ends up by bringing about a fabulous awareness: my clients realize that their partner wasn't indispensable, better yet, they often see how their presence made them unhappy.

"Do you promise?" I can, indeed. "Do you promise that this inhuman pain will soon make way for peace?"

Experience proves it, I'm positive.

The brain is endowed with a neuronal plasticity that we can shape as much as we want. If the emotion that comes from a memory can fade in forty days, it's easy to understand no man is essential. Neither the university soccer team captain nor the hot executive at the coffee machine or the ten years wedded man you thought you could never leave. And if none of them have managed to satisfy his partner the way he should have, let him go and no one will cry over him.

"I promise."

She stares at me as if she is searching for the truth of my statements.

My gaze is penetrating and confident. I don't bat an eye to reassure her. Even better, I try to spiritually shower her with this combativeness which imbibes every part of my being and which she will need to move forward.

After many seconds of hesitation, she nods to agree.

Doubt seems to be dispelled.

I give her a faint smile.

At last, she pulls out a tissue from her box.

She wipes off her face, takes off her wedding ring which she sets down on the table near to the mascara stained tissue, and she lifts her head, ready to face, with dignity, this new future which so strongly fuels her concerns.

That's why I do this job. To shape women in my image: combative, proud, worthy, and respectable. One day, I will enroll them in an army of dress-suit feminists, that I will lead, and we will quite naturally reign at the top of the world.

CHAPTER 12

Tuesday, May 2nd, 9:00 p.m.

The Von Beck Gala, one of the most important social events of the year. Three hundred distinguished guests are expected to come to enjoy an exceptional dinner. The dress code is dark and elegant as the magnificent crystal setting in which all guests are immersed, and an army of three-piece suited waiters are carrying champagne glasses on silver trays. For the occasion, I'm wearing a Balmain backless black custom-made dress. It was given to me three months earlier along with my invitation. All the high society women are in my address book and they all want to have me at their receptions. Each week, I, therefore, receive a whole stack of invitations. From garden parties to private evenings, I have my pass and my name is delicately placed on all the most prestigious lists.

Half of the women who are present this evening are loyal clients. Some are heading CAC 40 businesses, others hold major positions in prestigious business firms, and there are also heirs and millionaires. Even though they have an isolated existence with their little paradise, they don't all understand this intriguing phenomenon which is love and I am often the answer to their questions.

"Baroness, here you are at last!"

"Catherine…" An influential fifty-years old woman of the Parisian bourgeoisie, cheerfully joining my circle.

"I'm borrowing her for a minute." She takes me away from her peers by gripping my arm, I feel just as desired as a Balenciaga. "I couldn't wait to show you my new look. What do you think?"

I look at her bemused, I hadn't recommended a Halloween costume.

"Who did your makeover?"

"A boho, from the Marais district, with slightly off-the-wall tastes," she confesses with contentment.

"You have to remain faithful to your personality, Catherine, that's the secret of a successful makeover."

"Don't you like it?"

"Let's just say that I'm not very keen…"… on Lady Gaga's exuberance.

"You nevertheless advised me to add a touch of originality to my dress style."

"Some denim, possibly leather…" Certainly not a frilled neckline which would clearly highlight her tuberous bust. "It doesn't matter, call my assistant tomorrow." Sophie will take care of the problem.

"You're a sweetheart!" She should wait for my invoice before making that assertion. "You're always so useful… " she whispers while holding my hand. I don't know why sisterhood always turns into lesbianism. "By the way, let me introduce you to our host, Diane…"… Von Beck. The wife of the very wealthy Charles Von Beck, founder of the world's largest cosmetic empire. She is talking nearby with prominent businessmen in tuxedos. Our tuberous friend interferes once again. "Diane, here's our very dear Baroness."

She hastily turns around and throws her arms around me without bothering to salute her guests.

"Baroness, I've heard so much about you!" The tuberous slips away with a blissful smile on her lips. "And at last, you're honoring me with your presence!"

"The honor is mine to have been invited to such a sumptuous reception."

"Oh, please make yourself at home!" The high society always flatters me with such fervor. "Your commitment to teaching our sisters how to prevent abuse and misconduct from men is such a noble enterprise. How could we thank you for all that dedication to our community, if it isn't by giving you the honor and gratitude that you deserve."

"I'm just doing my job."

A job that buries me under women's cases, each one as nutty as the other. That indeed deserves honors, praise, and gratification.

"And so humble on top of that!" Her eyes twinkle and she caresses my arm. We might as well go straight to her place. "Would you be available for brunch, this Sunday?"

"I'm truly sorry, my schedule is full."

"What a shame!" She fiddles with her necklace. "My husband Charles…" To whom she owes her luxurious lifestyle. "… hasn't been himself lately."

She wants to divorce and take half the loot.

"Contact my assistant, we'll find you a slot."

"Wonderful!"

"Baroness, Diane…"

"Elisabeth…" One of the most powerful investigating judges in France.

"May I have a word, Baroness?"

Diane frowns.

"We're already in the middle of a conversation…!"

"This won't take long."

"Regardless, it remains totally inappropriate to cut off a conversation and even more to butt in without having been invited!"

Brawls always start this way, it might be time to intervene.

"Diane, I'm sure I'll have the pleasure of seeing you later this evening."

Such manna can't be ignored.

"You're so popular my dear, I'm delighted to have put you at my table."

She glares at her rival and reluctantly steps away.

"Elisabeth, your presence delights me."

We're going to be able to talk business.

"I didn't have the chance to see you at our last meeting, Baroness…"

The one of a secret feminist organization that gathers some of the most powerful women in France. Obviously, I'm the president.

"An infidelity case prevented me."

"Precisely, I received the latest ones. Do I need to rule again for the maximum penalty?"

For all the unfaithful husbands who evade the tax system…

"It's only fair."

"I'll grant you that."

These wealthy men who believe they're above state and nuptial laws are my life's obsession.

"We will successively crush them until there are none left."

"I like your pugnacity, Baroness, it promises such brighter days for all these wronged women!"

It's just a matter of time before all these boneheads understand that the rules of the game have changed.

"I'm pleased to contribute."

"If only I could have met you a few years earlier!" She would have known what to do with her doormat ex-husband.

"Have no regrets, the power is now in our hands, we'll use it wisely."

I raise my glass of champagne and we toast to spell the end of all accursed men who blithely take advantage of women's emotional weakness.

CHAPTER 13

Tuesday, May 2nd, 11:00 p.m.

"Ladies… " one of the few men able to make me smile interrupts. "Can I join you?"

"Elisabeth, let me introduce you to Louis Beaumont, the man of my life."

More specifically, a handsome six-foot-tall blond man with green eyes who I saw for the first time at a charity gala. He made a colossal six-figure check donation and after having enquired about the precise amount of his fortune, I decided to make him my new emotional project.

"What a lovely surprise!" Did she think I was a lesbian? "Aren't you Helene's and Richard's son?"

The Beaumonts are one of the richest families of France, integrating their clan will allow me to enhance my image so much more.

"Indeed."

"I knew you when you were a child and now you're so grown." She stares at him, even though she's too old for that. "How did you meet?"

Officially…

"At an auction."

He bites his lower lip, he's undoubtedly recalling the

memories of our first encounter. It's true that it was a totally successful phishing phase.

"She outbid me on a Van Gogh." Which I had no intention of buying and which he ended up offering me. "Two years later, here we are…"

"Married?"

I firmly anticipate with a simple…

"No."

But as he looks at me smiling, it probably won't be far off.

"Well, what are you waiting for to marry her?"

"To tell the truth, our schedules haven't yet allowed us to think it over."

"What's this job, which is so time-consuming, that it keeps you from marrying such a woman?"

"I'm heading a European investment fund." He handles millions while traveling between European capitals. I, therefore, enjoy being united to a real catch without having to daily overdo my feelings. " And I just got back from a business trip to London."

He takes my hand and looks at me lovingly. I usually just need to do likewise to make him happy. That's what we call NLP synchronization. Reproducing your companion's gesture will allow him to feel in total harmony with you. That said, my approach is not entirely devoid of sincerity since I admit that I am profusely in love with his bank account.

"We haven't seen each other for three days…" And I can't wait to find out if his financial assets have increased.

"Three days without her have seemed like an eternity."

I'm counting on our law expert's foresight to guess his irrepressible desire to savor our reunion.

"Don't say any more!"

She salutes us by nodding and finally ends up by leaving.

He'll have a chance to explain to me, among other things, why he's an hour late.

"I missed you," he whispers while holding me tight.

Should that excuse him?

"Where have you been?"

"I had to make a stopover in Geneva."

It's the sixth time this month.

"Should I worry?"

"You know how business is."

"Your pupils are dilating…" How dare he lie to me?

"What should I conclude?" That it might be time for me to tail him again. I had stopped a few months ago, out of laziness to listen to all those boring stock exchange phone conversations, but it's clearly a monumental mistake. Men are as deceitful as women, I should never have let that idea go. "Don't you trust me?"

I raise my eyebrows, how could he never have noticed that? Our relationship has always been codified by a multitude of principles, among which the formal prohibition for him to meet contacts I don't know about or the fact that he remains with a woman in a confined and isolated area.

Mathematic reasoning: the less he communicates with women, the smaller the risk of him leaving one day. I, therefore, took charge of all his social contacts and everything has been arranged so that I can have control over our entire relationship, which up to now was bordered by my omnipresence and whose positive direction was nothing more than the result of my own designs. How would things be if I had left him unattended?

"Trust is fundamental in a relationship, though."

To others!

"It's the sixth time you're late this month, with no other

valid explanation that a time-consuming business schedule. How should I take it?"

His phone rings, he lets go of me.

"It's Paul." His driver, but he answers with such eagerness that I end up thinking it's a potential *Paula*. I stalk enough creeps to know how this kind of nonchalant behavior can be indicative of perfidy. "Honey, I'll be back!"

Really?!

"In the middle of a conversation?!"

"I won't be long!"

He hurries off but he'll get what's coming to him!

A high-speed chase starts.

I run after him down the large reception room steps that lead outside.

I won't be one of those permissive clients who consistently pay no heed to their companion's misbehavior. He'll end up, willingly or not, giving me the respect I'm entitled to as a woman.

There he is, getting into his sedan far away. The tinted windows don't reveal any shadow of a mistress, but such minor detail has never stopped my impetuosity.

I brutally open the back door and find him… alone?!

"The only thing I'm guilty of is being madly in love with you!" I don't understand… "Get in, you'll catch a cold!" I sit next to him and *Paula* gets out of the sedan to discreetly stand away. "You were not supposed to join me here."

"If you hadn't been so taciturn, I wouldn't have had to."

"You always ruin everything with your impulsiveness," he says as he draws his face close to mine to contemplate each detail composing it. "But perhaps deep down that's what makes me so crazy about you," he concludes before gently biting my lower lip.

I push him away with my hand on his chest, what about that late arrival?

"Will I finally get some explanations?"

"Do you want the truth?"

If he cheated on me, I'll make his life a living hell!

"You know that I can't bear hidden faults." Nor that considerable amount of time that he's taking to bring me this damn truth!

"I wasn't in Geneva for business," he confesses, not daring look at me. Why the hell did I stop spying on him? "I was there to see a great jeweler." His pupils are dilating again but his nostrils as well, it's not a lie anymore but a physiological reaction reflecting his desire for me. "And each of my late arrivals is due to my several trips in this jewelry store because I wanted it as perfect as you are." He takes out a black jewel box case from his tuxedo's interior pocket. How could I ever doubt him? Since we've met, I've set a whole multitude of devious tricks to configure him precisely so that he ends up giving me that engagement ring. "When I saw you for the first time, I was immediately in love with you." Like they are all, obviously. "You were everything a man can dream of." Beautiful, smart, charismatic…, and what if he tried telling me something new. "And I didn't realize how lonely I was until I met you." I pull some tender expressions; high school drama classes will have the merit of being useful. "Now, I'm sure I have found the woman who I can't live without." He opens his jewel case and lets out, at last, a splendid solitaire ring, most certainly set with a four-carat diamond. It will perfectly match my luxurious wardrobe. "So, I'm solemnly asking you to be mine for the rest of your life."

"My love, how can I refuse?" The union of two capitalists inevitably promises a bright future. "Since I met you…" And his eight-figure bank account. "… my life has lightened up. How could I ever imagine living with someone else?" I get close to him and place my hands on his smooth cheeks. "I will be yours for the rest of our life."

"You're therefore making me one of the happiest men in the world." He gently puts the ring on my left ring finger, holds me tight as a symbol of marriage sacred bonds, and seals our union with a languorous kiss. As many actions predicted two years earlier at the auction. Except for the high-speed chase but let's not forget that even the most elaborate plans can contain miscalculations. "This proposal could have been more romantic but you caught me off-guard."

"What had you planned?"

"We were supposed to walk up to the rooftop of the reception room."

"Well, let's go."

I'll be able to proudly display my engagement ring to the wide world and show how the seduction expert handles her romantic relationships.

He hastily gets out of the sedan and walks around to open the door for me.

"If Madame Beaumont would be so kind…"

He offers me his hand, I take it to get out.

Holding his arm, I elegantly raise my dress with my left hand and point my brand new diamond toward the front to highlight it even more.

After proudly climbing the atrium stairs, we cross the reception room.

I see Chloe who raises her glass to congratulate me. I smile, give her a wink, and turn my head to the side.

My fiancé whispers sweet words in my ear. I pretend I'm charmed but tonight, only the Parisian high society's admiring eyes hold interest. They are my revenge for a circle that I had so much trouble integrating. Aware of the excitement I arouse, I proudly arch my back, with the idea, that this royal image will be forever engraved in the memory of the high-society.

A decor worthy of a royal palace was installed on the roof. Baccarat crystal lights trim a small path strewn with white roses, which leads to a table with a bottle of champagne and a porcelain saucer of caviar.

Louis smiles radiantly and gets down on one knee to kiss my hand. Close to my thirtieth birthday, a bank account in the Bahamas and a marriage proposal under a starry sky are all that I had imagined.

CHAPTER 14

Wednesday, May 3rd, 7:00 a.m.

There will be no alarm clock this morning. Yesterday night was so busy, promises of eternity, pillow talk, wild sexuality… the humid sheets will have a very hard time forgetting about it. I may well have no feelings for Louis, the sexual awakening he provokes in me holds no comparison. This probably due to the fact that he detains everything that can excite me: wealth, power, nobility. So many points that constitute what I have always worked to achieve.

He's still sleeping. I run my hand on his chest and put my head on his shoulder. He will wake up as satisfied as he was when falling asleep. Oh… something suddenly moves under the sheets, he's probably dreaming of me. I slide my hand along his abdomen for more realism.

"Good morning, my love," he breathes, his voice hoarse.

"Did you have a good night?" I murmur as my hand travels up his photoshopped chest.

"Your treats will end up killing me…"

When we are married, he will be continuously deluged with them. To maintain a man under sexual influence remains one of the surest ways of securing his attachment. At each intercourse, the brain releases an oxytocin secretion that automatically creates a new desire for the person provoking it. It, therefore, takes very little to dominate them.

I sit on the edge of the bed and wrap myself in a sheet.

"Join me in the shower," I whisper to excite him.

I turn around to scrutinize him; his eyes are full of desire.

"Do you have other plans?"

We are engaged, I want him to remember that eternally.

"Pull yourself together first," I suggest as I lean on him.

I surreptitiously kiss his lips and bite them softly.

"Should I take the day off?"

"I will do so as well." And this, for the first time of the year. "After all, aren't we engaged?"

With all that this implies in terms of fuss and new arrangements, each other's lives will now be different in many ways. My clients will be the first to notice it. I asked Marie to postpone all my appointments and increase my fees. My stage performance at the Von Beck gala has undeniably boosted my popularity. Not only am I the seduction expert, but also, this powerful woman masterfully leading her life that all will, tomorrow more than yesterday, want to know the secrets. So, let's take advantage of it.

I rush to the bathroom to gaze at the imposing woman I have, so majestically, become. I stay there, fixed, trying to become conscious of each element forming my identity: my appearance, my personality, my intellect, my profession, my finances, and my material possessions. I am soothed by a feeling of satisfaction. Today, I like my life. I find it beautiful, fulfilling, balanced, and it perfectly matches the ideal representation I had of it a few years earlier. It is nice. I have worked for a long time to achieve that. I, therefore, see it as a really good return on investment and I strive to become conscious of it.

I consider that nothing positive that has happened to me was a mere coincidence. On the contrary, my life is the result of a perfect meticulousness and as for an architectural project, I have conceived those plans and implemented them. I have dreamt of a brilliant career, business trips, a well-fed bank account, drinks with friends, and love that, since not finding it, I traded for Louis, a man who could wonderfully fit this sumptuous life set, that took me so much time to draw. I chose him on a description. The amount of his wealth was as important as his three-piece suits and his Italian shoes. They match my tailor-made suits and my sharp stilettos and are the ideal fashion accessories for me to make an impression. It is all a matter of appearance and the future we have started shaping, yesterday evening, will be even more so.

First of all, our wedding ceremony. It will be held next spring, in one of the greatest castles of France, listed as a historical monument: Vaux-le-Vicomte castle. We will hire "Sarah Baywood", one of the most renown "wedding planners" there is. A great fashion designer will create my wedding gown that I imagine made of satin, close-fitted with a bustier, and about five hundred selected guests will be able to admire me as they enjoy refined cuisine and great vintage wines.

We will then leave for our honeymoon, on a private jet. I will sensually inebriate my spouse at Lake Como, and abound his libido in the Caribbean Islands with countless nights of torrid lovemaking.

As soon as we are back, we will move in a vast private mansion of the good Paris. It will have beautiful ceiling heights, moldings, and an annex house for staff, including a typically French Chef.

Last, I will invest part of my time in a potential progeny, that will mark my belonging to the Beaumont family for good.

I will sign them in private schools, they will get private lessons in English and Japanese, and will ride horses do archery and swimming, as they will meddle in high society circles. Since every detail count, in this appearance world of which I am the Queen.

CHAPTER 15

Thursday, May 4th, 9:00 a.m.

"**G**ood morning, Baroness!"

"Good morning, Marie."

"Here's your glass of champagne, your messages, and your schedule for the day."

"I'm listening, Marie."

"Diane Von Beck asks for an appointment, you have received two hundred congratulation messages, among which thirty potential clients asking for a first consult. You'll see Sarah Baywood at 3:00 p.m. and the Rolex boutique manager is already in your office, in which I have set the five thousand white roses your fiancé had delivered for you this morning."

"Thank you, Marie."

"I would also like to give you my best wishes of happiness," she says shyly, blushing.

"That's so sweet."

Even if she doesn't mean a single word of that. Marie has always been crazily in love with me, I perfectly know the news isn't pleasant to her or to all those other dreamers that went by in my life, naïvely hoping to settle in. I really take pity on them.

I drink a sip of champagne and enter my office. Louis' white roses fill the space. It reminds me of my twenty-ninth birthday in Monaco, the non-stop delivery ballet that he had orchestrated. Each of his initiatives comforts me, each day a little more, on my choice, spending my life with him, promises he will not neglect any aspect of it. Hence the value of tracking him. I have decided to reopen his file to make sure he never leaves. Mathilde, who is comfortably seated in one of the leather sofas of the lounge area, is there to help. She's the manager of the Rolex boutique and will take charge of an important aspect of the tracking process, first consisting in placing a tracker in a Rolex.

"Mathilde!"

She puts her coffee cup on the table and rushes to salute me.

"I won't ask how you're doing, you are glowing with happiness!"

"That's the power of love…"… of success, money and incidentally of a Terracotta Touch on the cheekbones.

"Show me your solitaire," she begs, taking my hand. Her eyes sparkle, she probably never saw anything as sumptuous. "A four-carats that will perfectly match your luxury wardrobe!"

I smile widely, her sharp instinct delights me as much as this beautiful diamond.

"Let's sit." Face to face, on the sofas. "We have so much to tell each other."

Starting with this wedding proposal that makes them all dream.

"So tell me, how did he propose?" she asks curiously.

"Kneeling on a white rose flowered floor, illuminated with Baccarat crystal."

Let's skip the details of the high-speed chase that holds nothing glamorous.

"And his declaration?"

"Filled with compliments for me, without whom, and I quote, he wouldn't be able to exist."

"You're making me dream!"

Why not go on? She amuses me so much!

"I spent the whole night in his arms, did I mention?"

"And are all those roses from him?" she pries, amazed.

"I can't hide anything from you!"

She frowns, crosses her arms, and leans her head on the side.

"How do you tame him?" Am I not the seduction expert? "Thomas never showed the littlest sign of affection!" Which I don't ignore, his wedding vows have been bought. "What are your secrets?"

Why is she comparing us?

"You're aware that the circumstances are different."

"I forgot your profession!" And my identity. "Are you conscious of being one of the most powerful women of the Parisian high-society?"

"Can one escape his fate?"

"Of course not, you were born for this!" I never doubted that. "I knew what kind of woman you were the moment you set foot in my boutique." Five years earlier, to buy my first Rolex. "You were so bold!" In a social circle were women limit themselves to show reserve, I appeared as the exception outrageously copulating with the rule. "You introduced yourself as the deal of the century and left me your card adding that I would certainly need your services."

"And since then, you haven't been able to do without them."

She's had her husband traced for the past five years with no strength to stop.

"How could I?" She's as addicted to my services as she is to antidepressants. "I certainly hope you're not considering quitting?"

What an absurd idea.

"Why would I?"

"You could have other ambitions."

"What could be more noble…" … and profitable… "… than the feminine cause?"

We frown.

"Didn't it occur to you to get involved in the Beaumonts family enterprises?"

"Vanish for the benefit of my spouse?" Me, the inveterate feminist? "Certainly not!"

A smile of blissful admiration endows her face.

"You command such respect."

"And even more in the future, since my wedding will not cut my appetite. On the contrary, I intend to use it to reach my goals." I finish my glass of champagne and continue unabated. "I want to develop my customer base, expand my network, and the members of my feminist association will be much more elitist."

Beaumont's address book overflows with gems.

"What do you mean?"

I'm intriguing her.

"Congresswomen, State Secretaries, members of the European Parliament, who knows how things could evolve if I could bond with the most powerful female politicians?"

"You'd probably end up at the White House."

I graciously cross my legs and run my fingers through my hair.

"The Baroness is highly worth it."

"I have the feeling that I won't come back to this office anytime soon, you'll fast renew your address book and forget about me. Have your assistant bring me another of those delicious coffees, I'd like to enjoy it."

"Don't be foolish and show me what you brought." A steel briefcase holding close to half a million euros of luxury watches. I look at mine, it's getting late. "Marie, have Yuri come in and secure the premises."

Doors will be locked, emergency exits will be blocked, and Yuri will stand at my office door weapon in hand until the operation is concluded.

"Promise me it won't be the last," Mathilde asks, fearful, before putting the briefcase on the table separating the two sofas.

Thus, she reminds me of how devoted the members of my association are to me. Out of sorority, they climb mountains. They plot, lie, cheat, are involved in secret operations that could cost them their career, their marriages, their reputations as quiet and settled women; but it doesn't matter, in their eyes there's nothing like the adrenaline that the feminine reign I provide them offers and that money itself couldn't buy.

"I will invite you to the White House," I assert in a serious tone to comfort her.

"I was expecting no less of you!" she exclaims as she enters a code on the numeric keyboard of the briefcase.

She carefully opens it and turns it my way.

I come closer for better visibility.

My eyes wander about but I remain skeptical.

Louis owns almost all of them.

"What are the novelties?"

She bends her head and shows me a steel watch with a red and blue ceramic face.

"The Oyster Perpetual GMT-Master II."

I pull it out of its velvet base and meticulously watch it.

"He adores steel watches."

"He has good taste."

I raise my eyebrows. Who could doubt that in view of the bombshell he's engaged with?

"But that's not the question, I mainly see that he'll be able to wear it every day, along with my tracker."

"The point is relevant."

As is the choice.

"I'll take it."

"Do you want to have his initials engraved?"

"Rather love words."

Since it's a poisoned chalice, let's make it remarkable.

"Which ones?" she asks while taking a pen and notebook from her bag.

"For life, B.,"

She writes them down and smiles broadly.

"It's cute."

Enough intense romanticism.

"Talk to me about the installation process," I command firmly to cut her cheerfulness.

My seriousness instantly imposes her to get back to hers.

"First, you'll be glad to see that Rolex has created a new mechanical movement: the caliber 3255. It is made of phosphorus-nickel, which makes it insensitive to magnetic disturbances."

She hands me a brochure.

I briefly look over it and put it on the table.

"It is an insulating material?"

"That perfectly works to shelter an electronic device such

as your tracker, that, I'd like to point out, will have to weigh less than 18 grams."

"For what reasons?"

"All watches are subject to a very strict quality charter when it comes to weight and dimensions."

"It will then weigh 17 grams." For more safety. "When will it be inserted?"

"After a series of tests. The Rolex gets to engraving after the quality control. It's being inserted between those two steps, it's the safest way to avoid being caught."

"What about delays?"

"You can plan on 72 hours tops."

"It's way too much. I'm having dinner at Louis' parents soon, I need it before that."

"It's doable if I go to the Swiss workshop tonight."

"Do you have reliable contacts there?"

"Two loyal friends I studied with, in Lausanne."

"You'll have to send me their contact details, I'd like to know how I'm dealing with."

"Have no fear, they're as feminist as we are. By the way, one of them wanted to call on your services, you'd do me a favor by treating her as a priority."

"Let's not put the cart before the horse."

"Your Rolex, consider it done," she asserts as she carefully closes the briefcase. We stand up. "I'll keep you informed on the operation's progress."

"Perfect."

"And on your side, if things weren't going well with Thomas…" she worries.

"Don't trouble yourself."

"You'd tell me…"

… if her husband cheated on her with a big chested blonde answering to the deliciously pornographic name of Carla?

"You can count on me!"

CHAPTER 16

Thursday, May 4th, 10:00 a.m.

I convened my assistants in my office. Sophie is seated on
the sofa, Marie is next to her, standing, tablet in the hand
to take note of my instructions. My wedding entices me
to make countless changes which enumeration will take place
this morning.

"Marie, starting tomorrow, you'll wear tailored suits and
you'll throw away your filthy plastic flats." A bit of esthetics
won't hurt. "Sophie, don't look at me like that, it's also for you.
I don't want to see your rangers anymore."

"How do I do on the field?"

"You'll find much more classy boots at Balmain." Their
dumbstruck look doesn't surprise me the least. Low-grade
staff rarely integrates the colossal stakes resulting from modest
changes. "That's not all, exit clients with dental braces, scared
virgins, and managers whose annual income doesn't exceed
100K per year."

"What about pro bono?" Marie asks meekly.

To hell with philanthropy.

"The firms' turnaround must exceed one million by the
end of the year." Today, I'm a businesswoman, it's about time
to act accordingly. "You'll close my social network pages." It

is no longer useful to win the favor of the acneic students. "Philanthropy is over!"

"And how should we announce it?" Marie continues as she passionately takes notes of my orders.

"I'll post a status in my spare time." Something like: all good things come to an end except for me. This type of sentence always makes a little effect on young girls scarred by seborrhea. "Meanwhile, book a shooting at Harcourt Studios, we'll use the photos for the new corporate communication to be deployed after the wedding."

"Which one?" Sophie asks, frowning questioningly at me.

I frown too, seriously?

"Aren't you aware?" All the city is. "I'm engaged, haven't you noticed this splendid diamond ring I proudly display?" I show it to her. She seems flabbergasted. "Hasn't Marie told you about it?"

I glare at her with disapproval.

"Sorry, I didn't get the chance to," she admits shyly.

That goes to say daydreaming is a time-consuming activity.

"Well then, go back to your occupations," I command firmly, implacable.

She blushes, puts her head down to hide her flushed face, and leaves on tip-toe. It's generally the effect I have.

"So, you're engaged?" Sophie resumes as she still seems to be processing the news.

"What's so surprising?"

"I don't know, I thought you were against all forms of institution."

Not if I lead them, also…

"Marriage is just a formality."

Between two legal entities consenting to live in the same house, to have a roll in the hay and to strike a pose in public from time to time. As for me, for a solid fee of a few hundred million euros.

"B., I've been married twice…" To two hicks, one of which was jobless. "… it's anything but a formality."

"For your information, my fiancé is from one of the wealthiest families in France."

No doubt she will end up realizing we don't evolve in the same circles.

"Do you intend to join his company?"

What's with them all on this?

"This is the 21st century, women don't need to exist through their husbands, this is all over." And I ensure the continuity of this empowerment.

"Then, why the upheaval?"

"It's a corporate reshuffle." But once again, I don't expect the little people to understand the meaning of my words. "I am now one of the most influential women in France and my wedding will give me more leverage. It's important to reshape the firm so it can be more in line with my image."

"I thought you were going to close the business."

"You're in my kingdom, the day I'll close the business I'll be dead and buried."

"So, I'll keep my job?"

"I'm announcing my engagement and that's all that matters to you?" She's embarrassed. How not to be? "You didn't even wish me the best!"

"You know well I hate marriage…"

Celebrating it in a cheap venue certainly leaves a bitter taste.

"Be assured mine will be different." In many ways. "I'm the seduction expert, don't ever forget it." I point out a file on the table. "To refresh your memory."

She takes it.

"Who's the client?"

"The Popess of Parisian high society, who is no other than me." It is true that one marriage out of two generally ends up in a divorce. I refuse to be on the wrong side of the fence. I have already managed to overcome many obstacles to couple's longevity, among which cellulite, stretch marks, and abdominal fat, today I radically take care of infidelities. "My fiancé Louis Gerald Beaumont, an extremely rich businessman with a model figure, regularly rubs shoulders with voracious women. The primary idea is to identify those who, over time, could be an issue: assistants, subordinates, clients. To be clear, all those intensely gravitating in his orbit." We'll redirect all coquettish e-mails to our server and telephone calls will not follow through.

"Do we deport them to new life trajectories?"

"Of course, each of them is concerned. We clean up, 3.0 update." We'll have all the bombshell fired for professional fault and will replace them with Ugly Bettys. I ponder: I should never have stopped tracking him. "Who knows how many Barbie have entered his life since?"

"There must be a whole battalion of them," Sophie says ironically while she takes notes.

"Add to that, that my case takes priority and that the deadline is set for the end of the year."

"That's the wedding date?"

"It hasn't been scheduled yet but next spring seems to be the most plausible."

Before that, I have so much to do, from preparations to corporate reshuffle, going through the new communication plan, and Louis' tracking file.

"We have a year to take care of it, don't you think it's plenty of time?"

"You can never be too careful." Especially since the tracking particularly bothers me. "You'll set trackers in his cars, the lining of his suits, and the sole of his shoes." Because no one is more Machiavellian than a woman willing to keep her man for herself. "Don't forget the spy software, including in his assistant's computers."

"And his watch?"

"Mathilde is taking care of it."

"Passwords?"

"Everything is in the file." The plans of his house, the alarm codes, his IDs, and his spare key. "For information, he leaves his place at 7:00 a.m., the cleaning ladies arrive at 7:30 a.m., you have a very short window to do the job."

"I'll divide it up, she informs with a crooked smile." Her cerebral nut never prevents her from doing her job in standard practice. "I saw that you canceled all your appointments for the week?" she continues more seriously.

"The days to come will be busy for everyone, it's pointless to overload them."

"I still have three cheated wives ongoing in addition to Camille Meyer."

"I told you, my file comes in priority, I don't want any other irons on the fire."

"And what am I supposed to do with them?"

"Delegate." She only has to send them to shrinks. "Is it all good for you?"

"It's all very clear."

"Well then Private, dismiss," I command satisfied.

I found Sophie on a military reserve list. A young twenty-five years old athlete, with an adequate profile: patriotic, daring, brave, loyal, and of which frustration to be unable to put her skills to profit had ended up pushing her to alcoholism. Our encounter couldn't be more appropriate. I had just opened my consulting firm and was looking, all in the same time, for psychologically unstable subalterns which chaotic lives held nothing more than the unbearable wait for an opportunity, and feminists in quest of adventures and ideals who could agree to everything I'd order. Following the example of Marie, who went from one speed dating to another in search for the great love, that she would only find, at last, in me.

"Baroness, your fiancé is on the phone," she breathes bitterly.

I sit at the desk and breathe with the same frustration.

I'm going to have to overdo it again.

"Hello, my love," I say with a velvety voice.

"My beauty!" He sounds relieved. "I thought you'd never answer!"

"Did you call me?"

"At least ten times!"

"I must have put my smartphone on silent mode, I'm overflowed with messages and calls since the gala." Not to mention the e-mails.

"Same for me."

"So, it's official?"

He won't be able to escape it anymore.

"I even called my parents to tell them," he declares cheerfully.

"How did they react?"

"Very well, they're thrilled." And they haven't seen me yet! "We'll have dinner at their place on Saturday evening," he continues joyfully.

What was I saying about that much talked about dinner?

Men are always in a hurry to introduce us to their parents. Saturday seems a little premature but…

"Perfect…"

"I'm sensing a small hesitation in your voice tone…"

"Not at all." The Beaumonts must be a charming senile old couple. A few salutations will be enough to please them. "I can't wait to meet them…"… to laugh at their stupid jokes and pretend I'm having a good evening.

"And your parents?" That we'll have to bring from their province. "Did you tell them?"

"I didn't have the time to." To say the truth, I more and more consider hiring actors to replace them and to whom I'd teach a few high society lessons. My parents are so far from those codes. They would probably be discordant in that new decor, better not to humiliate them and me, by the way. "But rest assured, I'm thinking about it."

"Hurry up, time is of the essence."

"That's why I meet our wedding planner today."

"Can you postpone? I don't think I can make it."

Who said he was invited?

"My love…" Nth manipulation lesson: always punctuate commanding sentences with affectionate words, to counterbalance their rhythm. "… your presence isn't required." Or wanted, or desirable. "I will know how to handle it." What I call my wedding and not his.

"Very well," he concedes with a gloomy voice dragging a long deafening silence, symptomatic of disappointment.

Maybe he was expecting a teamwork as all engaged couples do? What for? Let's rather change the subject.

"I received your roses, I'm fulfilled."

"Too bad my involvement in the wedding is limited to flowers."

"To me, it's plenty."

"Okay, I have to go, I'm boarding," our minx says as *she* hangs up on me.

He'll end up paying for it.

Meanwhile…

"Marie, add the Beaumonts to my address book and redirect their calls to voicemail."

If the mother is as tortured as the son, she'll constantly call to chat and I keep those attentions to a very limited number of privileged people, among which Chloe, with whom I haven't had a chance to talk since the gala. Power is a busy occupation that doesn't leave much time for frolics. Luckily, I now have a few minutes to gossip.

"So, how does it feel to be engaged?"

"Well, I feel richer of a few million euros."

"And you didn't even forget about me!"

"I actually thought about it."

But then, who would jigger my taxes?

"You still need me, don't you?"

"No joke, I haven't stopped since this morning."

"Wasn't it what you wanted?"

"You know me so well."

"At least enough to know how much you're gloating."

I smile broadly.

"Worse, I exult. My popularity rating is up by *44%* and requests don't stop flowing in. Louis is one of the most profitable investments I've made in my whole life."

"In the absence of love…"

"… might as well have the money." We laugh in unison. As materialists, everything is so obvious. "By the way, I'll make the transaction official next spring. Needless to add that you'll be my bridesmaid."

"I already knew that. Who organizes it?"

"Sarah Baywood, I have a 3:00 p.m."

"That doesn't surprise me either."

"I am the queen of pageantry, could it have been otherwise?"

"What does your fiancé think about it?"

"Who cares?"

"At least, you stayed true to your feminist principles."

"More than ever, I reopened his file, from now on he won't have any room left for maneuver. He'll content himself with signing checks and I won't oppose to a few necessary rolls in the hay to my mental health…"… and essential to the success of any relationship. "Can you imagine he dared to hang up on me?"

"No joke?"

I fly off the handle.

"That's the result when you unleash a mad dog!"

"Don't forget that animal abuse is severely punished."

"Too late, he's back in the cage."

He should never have gotten out of it.

"That's where we like them!"

"And nowhere else!" Anyway. "Do you want to have lunch with me at the office?"

"Why not?"

"Perfect, I'll order Japanese."

CHAPTER 17

Thursday, May 4th, 2:55 p.m.

The lunch set me on fire.

My private moments with Chloe always make me more vehement than I usually am. The fact that she encourages my high jinks probably has a lot to do with it. With her, I re-paint the world my own way and she cheers on every color, however dark they may be. What a powerful stimulant. I suddenly don't want to leave her anymore.

"I'll come back!" she shouts as she rushes out the doorstep.

Unbuttoned jeans shirt, barely closed luxury bag, Wayfarers on her head, and cigarette in the hand ready to burn. The tax advisor leaves a bit dowdy, without caring too much about it. There's much more important, she's late. Our endless conversations often push us to be for appointments following our reunions. The clock surreptitiously ticks under our sarcastic laughs and to be on time becomes an insurmountable challenge we never escape.

I sigh. Sarah Baywood is probably in the elevator. I just have time to freshen up.

I stand up and Marie comes in to clear our dishes.

"Prepare doggy bags for the homeless of the Vincennes woods," I exclaim haughtily as I gain my personal restroom.

Everybody has their own problems. As for me, I, critically, need a makeup touch-up and a little touch of woody notes perfume. Sushi smells are never really beneficial to first impressions and I don't make a habit of ruining mine.

CHAPTER 18

Thursday, May 4th, 3:00 p.m.

I'm glad.

Money can buy everything or anything, including the anticipated coming of one of the most demanded wedding planners in the world. She comes specifically from London and she is right on time.

"Thank you for coming on such short notice," I say politely as I welcome her at the office entrance.

"Thank you for your interest!" she replies, smiling warmly.

It is strange.

"You look very different from your website's pictures," I say, surprised while staring at her.

"Well since those pictures, a few pounds have been lost." I frown, wouldn't it be a solid ton of additional fat? "Between work and the kids, you know how it is…"

Here's what happens when you stuff yourself with wedding cakes.

"How was your flight?"

Did the airline make her book two seats? In which case, do her traveling expenses include those? I won't pay a dime for that. After all, I'm responsible for her coming, not for her excess weight.

"Perfectly!" she cuts while looking right and left. "What lovely roses you have here!"

"My fiancé had them delivered."

"So romantic, you'll ineluctably be a happy wife!" she exclaims, her eyes wide open.

"Most certainly…" Considering the weight of his wallet, which instantly reminds me of hers. I scratch my head. Where am I going to set her? No doubt the question deserves attention. She arrives with a gear as voluminous as her figure is: a strapped briefcase on the right shoulder, a suitcase she rolls in the left hand, and a bunch of binders and catalogs stuck under her arms. "Right here, please." The lounge area is furnished with two two-seater sofas and a tempered glass table of which strong materials will let her expand her cumbersome package (fat included) as she pleases.

"I heard about your services from a few French friends and I have to admit it's quite flattering to organize the wedding of a seduction expert," she confides while putting her jumble on the table.

"Well, I'm glad…" … to hear she's a potential future client.

"How lucky we are to live love every day!" she claims falsely.

It's so much more sales-worthy than to admit she has to pay the mortgage of her villa in Miami.

"Tell me about it!" I say ironically as Marie brings a tray of Darjeeling tea that she's struggling to put on the table.

"As for me, I took the liberty of bringing a signed copy of my book," she announces proudly, without guessing that we'll put it for sale on Amazon. "I teach about the art of wedding celebrations." With style, sophistication, and spirit… those are the words used on the back cover. I hadn't planned for her to be as conceited as I am. She already exhausts me! "You see, I mostly see myself as an artist who plans unique events for very special women." I don't give a damn!

"It's time to get to it."

"Don't you want to wait for your future husband?"

"It's not necessary." I'm the one wearing the G-string. "I'm handling the wedding preparations; my fiancé will take charge of the financial side of it. Here's his card for the details."

"Should I confer with him about our various packages?"

"Which are they?"

"Basic for small budgets, Middle for those wanting to treat themselves while keeping costs reasonable, and High Class for wealthier clients with no budget limits. Obviously, the bigger budget, the dreamiest wedding," she argues to lure me.

"My fiancé and I are worth a colossal fortune."

That she couldn't equal within a hundred lives.

"So, I guess you'll go with…"

"… High Class."

"You'll be glad to know that it includes the possibility of having renowned singers such as Ricky Martin, Jay-Z or Enrique Iglesias to perform."

I freeze and swallow my smile.

Do I look like I'd wriggle on Ricky Martin's songs?

"Paris Philharmonic Orchestra will be perfect."

We'll add Ed Sheeran to that and we'll leave the ceremony with a gold East Coast sound to tickle our guests.

"Let me take notes of that!" she gushes as she grabs her laptop. I take that moment to sip my tea. "I really appreciate to be able to create freely, with no budget constraints it's all simpler." My eyes unintentionally cling on her curvy fingers, I understand that no budget constraints mean all-you-can-eat cookies and buffet!

"It's not in my habits to be sticky on means."

"About that, how would you describe yourself?"

"As a perfectionist particularly versed in esthetics."

"I immediately spotted that when I got in your office, everything is so refined."

I smile crookedly.

She's far from having seen everything: my car, my house, my wardrobes, even the inside of my fridge where every condiment is set in a perfectly straight, symmetrical, and harmonious way.

"It goes without saying that my wedding must be equally sumptuous."

"Do you have an idea of what it could possibly look like?" To the detail. "Maybe a theme, a detail, scattered visions of what might delight you?"

"I imagined that the Paris Philharmonic Orchestra would open a royal and contemporary wedding taking place at Vaux-le-Vicomte Castle. My fiancé and I will cross the central alley in a black sedan and guests will be standing on the sides to admire our arrival. The banquet will take place outside. Round tables will be decorated with Baccarat crystal chandeliers, the crockery will be immaculate white, the cutlery will be silvered, and the flower arrangements will be composed of white roses, my favorite. We will have truffles, caviar, lobster, wine tasting, a column of vintage champagne glasses, and various sweets created by a renowned pastry chef. I already picked the caterer, the wedding gown, the shoes, my fiancé's tuxedo, his bouton-nière, and my diamond tiara created by Cartier. My assistant will give you their contact details. You'll just have to organize each of the aforesaid wishes," I say hastily without giving her time to intervene.

"Perfect…" she mumbles, choked up, after understanding

how much sweat and calories my demanding nature will cost her.

Was she actually expecting to supplant my creativity and genius? I laugh.

"Let's get to the 3D plans!" I command with arrogance, splendor, and vanity.

CHAPTER 19

Saturday, May 6th, 6:00 p.m.

This evening, I'm having dinner at the Beaumonts. I never had the opportunity to meet them. At best, I have caught sight of the mother at a few festivities. She's a very sophisticated woman displaying her jewels in galas, with no conscience of provoking dangerous desires of all those who, like me, want to board the golden ship. Tonight, she's inviting me to it with no objection. The solemn nature of the dinner requires me to wear a sober and elegant outfit, including a black dress with a thin grained leather belt. My hair is tied up, my make-up light, my perfume soft. I'm wearing my best smile and I bought an orchid bouquet. Helene Beaumont adores them, I googled her. This evening, everything will be staged, my manners, my expressions, my behaviors, and my emotions, since I'm rolling my dices on a hundred million table.

"Are you ready?" Louis asks coldly, with no tender look.

"More than ever," I respond dryly, remembering his insult.

We silently walk on the path between my house and his sedan.

Paul opens the back doors and we get in after another.

On the way, we both look out the windows, an awkward-ness sets in as kilometers go.

"Are you still mad?" I say, thinking of his checkbook. It can't slip out my hands. "Louis, we're getting married."

"It surely doesn't feel that way," he says harshly, staying still.

"May I know what raises such certainty?"

He turns to me and stares.

"You're the only one enjoying the pleasures of this wedding," he rebukes me childishly.

"Are you still mad that I didn't invite you to the meeting with Sarah Baywood?"

"I'm just wondering if you'll exclude me from all our married life."

What a question!

"My love, I didn't realize how important it was to you."

And didn't care one bit!

"After all, I'm only the groom!"

He hung up on me and dares to complain!

"Your schedule is so busy. Should I have imposed you to leave your ten million euros contracts to come and pick sugared almonds?"

"Do not blame my enthusiasm!"

"I'm not! I'm marrying the man I love, I'm happy, I'm over the moon! In the excitement, I thought I'd anticipate and so what? I simply thought it was for the best!" He hotly sighs and clenches his jaw. I sigh too and turn my back on him. "And if you can't see that…"… I'm using reverse psychology. "… what good does it to insist?"

"I just wish you thought about me," the emotional girl concludes.

"Louis, you are the center around which my life gravitates. You might not be always physically present but you never leave my heart and spirit." His face softens. "Understand now that this meeting was just a formality, I only exposed the points we'd already discussed." We were in the bedroom, one of the best places to impose ideas. "Do you remember? My wedding gown, made of satin, close-fitting with a bustier, refined dishes, unlimited vintage wines, the honeymoon, the mansion…"

His subconscious is filled with my wishes.

"You're probably right…" he admits while searching his memory.

"We've already talked about it, you just forgot."

"Of course, I remember now!"

"That you may have overreacted?"

"Please forgive me."

"You even hung up on me…"

"I'm so sorry!"

Dumb fool, next time, he'll kiss my toes to make amends!

CHAPTER 20

Saturday, May 6th, 7:20 p.m.

We arrive after more than a one-hour drive. The sedan enters in the driveway of an impressive mansion built on three floors. I forget all gripes and freeze fascinated by such opulence.

"Do you like it?" Louis asks.

I nod out of envy.

"One day, I'll have the same."

"That's the worst I wish for us," the simpleton says without noticing.

Have I included him in my project?

"Let's go, your parents must simmer with impatience," I say to divert.

Paul jumps by my words.

He rushes to open the door and salutes me as a sign of allegiance.

He acknowledges my preeminence at last!

The many heated conversations which I managed to get out of probably have a lot to do with it. A woman handling her man with such art and subtlety obviously inspires respect.

"Honey, take my purse," I command to twist the knife in the wound.

This evening, my ego is bursting. For sure, the in-laws will be amazed.

"You did well buying it!" Louis gushes while looking at my orchid's bouquet.

"I also have a gift for your father."

A bottle of vintage wine packaged in an engraved box, that I astutely won in an auction.

"I am sure they'll love you." Following the example of their son who still hasn't sated his love for me. "Now that we've made up, let me tell you how beautiful you are…" he whispers joyfully, taking me by the waist.

"You too, my love."

It is true that he's wearing everything I like: a white shirt, open at the collar, a pair of jeans, and brown leather Italian shoes.

"And I've missed your lips…" he adds as he kisses me passionately, on the doorstep.

"Not here, your parents could see us…"

"Then they'll know how crazy about you I am."

"Isn't our wedding formal proof of it?"

"Not to my mother, believe me!"

"Has someone called me?" a pinched-smiling sexagenarian, firmly standing at the entry door, says ironically.

"Darling, let me introduce you to my mother, Helene." Atrociously plumped with hyaluronic acid but still wearing an elegant grey shawl, ideally contrasting with a black velvet dress.

"Ms. Beaumont, I'm delighted to meet you," I flatter docilely, extending a hand she barely shakes.

"And how is my baby?"

"I've missed you!" he exclaims, with a long embrace.

An elevator music wouldn't have been too much for the

wait. I find myself so lonely with such familiarity, with my wine box and my orchids bouquet.

"Let me help you with those," mom-in-law offers without bothering to thank me. It was indeed worth buying them.

"The box is a gift for Richard," I explain to avoid her to toss it in the back of her cupboard.

"He shouldn't be long, get seated in the living room," she orders coldly as she rudely leaves.

Louis leads me in a large vestibule with a dark wood floor, leading to an immense living-room. I stare at the alluring luxury therein.

"The sofas were handcrafted by Italian artisans, the carpets have been woven in Hungary, the floor coverings come from Dalmatian forests… my parents didn't scrimp."

"When you have the money, why not go all the way?" I shout while sitting on the sofa that will be mine by inheritance, just like the house.

"What a lovely young woman!" dad-in-law interrupts a bottle of wine in hand.

"Richard!" Louis' father, a good-looking gentleman with a quite preserved hair capital, that I rush to salute. "I couldn't wait to meet you!" And to figure out what Louis would look like as an old man. "I'm very honored!" My investment is even better than I thought.

"Louis is full of praise for you," he informs while shaking his hand.

"And I could go on all day!" my fiancé adds to flatter me.

All those breeding hours will finally pay off!

"I'm afraid I won't escape that myself," dad-in-law confesses while admiring my bottle of wine.

"Please, it's such a small thing." Compared to what I'm going to enjoy.

"Wasn't it auctioned?"

"I'm the mystery buyer."

"That's a stubborn woman." With sharp and long teeth. "We'll savor it during dinner!" he concludes, his eyes sparkling with avidity.

CHAPTER 21

Saturday, May 6th, 8:00 p.m.

Amaid leads us to the dining room. A sumptuous meal is being served under a striking crystal chandelier and the table, covered with a crisp white linen tablecloth, is set, with silver candle rums. I take my place beside Louis, Richard is at the head of the table, and Helene, who imposes her damned presence again, is seated at the other end. I avoid any visual contact as I am remembering table manners, presuming she'd sneakily be watching me out of the corner of her eyes. My elbows are withdrawn, my back is straight, and Louis kisses me on the cheek at the most perfect time.

"Louis, darling, would you say grace?" she interrupts out of jealousy.

I smile wickedly before inclining my head as a sign of reverence. Tonight, I'm the guest of honor, whatever she may think of it. Her son picked me and nothing and nobody can change that.

"Amen!" we shout all together.

"Let's now enjoy the vintage wine you brought for us," dad-in-law suggests as he grabs the bottle. "And since you're our guest, I'll let you do the honors, Louis, please pour wine for your fiancée."

"If only she wishes to."

"I drink very little, a glass of champagne at the most on special occasions."

"Isn't your presence one?" Louis' mother shouts devilishly.

"Even more, it's a true boon. But my profession obliges me to keep an almost permanent sober state."

"And why is that?"

"My rationality must allow to channel the bitter emotionalism of my clients, for whom I must, according to a clause of our contracts, be available at any time."

"What exactly is your profession?" she continues insidiously. "Louis has been rather vague on the topic. Are you some sort of couple therapist?" Some sort?

"Not really, no… " Bitch! "… my profession is more much uncommon."

"Which means?" she strikes virulently.

For sure, I'll drill her eyes before the dinner ends.

"To say the truth, I handle love relationships of my clients through a multidisciplinary approach that entails consulting in natural habitat."

"I'm wondering…" she insists, women are so cruel. "How can a well-raised young woman dare infiltrate a married couples' privacy? And mostly, what do your parents say about it?"

"That's might be a matter of debate but my interest is purely altruistic. Many of our sisters are often overwhelmed by the state of events, not knowing how to handle their couples or lives. I take part in their lives in the sole goal to set them back on track." How boring! Louis and Richard have already given up. Luckily, they're discussing business and savoring a succulent roasted chicken. "In short, I'm just very moved by the feminine cause." As well as money.

"Do you approve of the vulgar and outrageous behavior of that feminist small group who stripes left and right in public events?" I frown. "What are they called? Flebloom? Flebleme?"

"Femen." Instrument of power, funded by a mysterious oligarchy in order to lessen the respectable image of women. "I hold nothing in common with them." No need to strip to reign. I do it with class and effectiveness. "Neither do I support their fanciful activities."

"That's at least good news," she says ironically while swallowing a bite. I'll be able to taste, at last. On the menu, roasted chicken, carrots, potatoes, and parsnip. My eyes are already savoring. "Did you have potatoes, Louis?"

"Twice, mom."

"Add a third to that," she orders coldly with an impassive expression.

An icy silence settles under the weight of her authority.

"Helene, the meal is delicious," I say to break it.

"Thank you for the caterer," she stings in a mocking and authoritative tone.

"My mother isn't very much of a cook either."

"And for what mysterious reasons couldn't she join us?"

"Well…" The confidentiality agreements that the actors have to sign aren't quite ready yet. "… it's all a matter of time, as usual."

"What is keeping your parents so busy?"

"Daddy currently manages one of the biggest shipyards of Europe, and Mommy handles its administration."

After all, one more lie won't hurt anybody, right?

"That's amazing, you should have told me!" Louis reproaches.

"It's not that interesting."

"Family businesses always are!" Richard gushes, probably thinking of his.

On second thought, my parents' enterprise is doing rather well. Dad is retired and sleeps in until 10:00 a.m., Mom is a housewife, she prepares his coffee and toasts. He tinkers with his old car until noon, snores in the afternoon, and enjoys the pleasures of tv-games at the end of the day.

"I wouldn't have the audacity to assert their business is as important and prestigious as yours, but it is the main reason for their absence."

"At a year from the wedding, we'll have plenty of time to meet them. I'll call your father to let him know our house is theirs." Richard concludes.

"Well, I'd like to propose a toast to that," I announce as I take my glass.

"With still water?" Satan criticizes.

Plan B will certainly end her causticity. I planned a bit of emotionalism to soften the assembly. At worst, if it doesn't work, there are still twenty six letters in the alphabet.

Everyone takes their glasses and I take a deep breath.

"Helene, Richard, I would like to thank you for welcoming me to your home and moreover your family." I tilt my head with the firm conviction that this staging will end up being awarded. "And I deeply regret that my parents couldn't join to see how loving and warm you are." And dull and naïve to the core.

"But the pleasure is ours!" Richard interrupts while tenderly looking at me.

If the audience is there, the artistic performance will follow.

"Louis, thank you for being the gentle man you are and for blessing my life in so many ways."

"My princess!" he exclaims as he voraciously kisses me in front of the dumbfounded eyes of his shrew mother.

"To you!" she shouts enraged.

"To your marital union, may it be fruitful and auspicious!" Richard exclaims, lifting his glass joyfully.

Satan drinks bottoms up to find some courage.

"Cheers!" I say, hoping she chokes!

CHAPTER 22

Saturday, May 6th, 9:30 p.m.

Dinner is coming to an end.

"Let's leave our men to their business conversations," The Mummy suggests while dragging me to the large and opulent living-room, that will be mine by inheritance, just like the house.

We seat, facing each other, on the sofas. If Louis wasn't in the next room I would fear that one of our two bodies disappear before the end of the evening.

"Will you have coffee?" she offers, smiling wickedly as she pours one for herself.

"No thank you, I'm not really a coffee person."

And I even less like it to be sprinkled with cyanide.

"Don't you have any kind of addiction?"

Aside from money?

"Not really, no."

"You seem to be a very balanced young woman."

Would she have abdicated?

"I'll take that as a compliment."

"I don't give them often."

"It's even more touching."

"Enjoy it," she says before haughtily sipping her coffee.

It seems her cruelty is revived.

"Would you have a few demands for the wedding?" I coax with a smooth voice, to suffocate it.

"Obviously, among which a tradition we keep, consisting in getting married at the abbey of Vaux-de-Cernay. The priest is a long-time friend, he'll bless your union."

"Well, I have to admit that I'm not very religious."

Neither is his son, considering what happens in the bedroom.

"I thought I guessed that by your profession."

"Neither am I a Catholic."

"We are!" she thunders. "And you'll wear, for this reason, a red pompom to mark your entrance in the family."

"Needless to say that I'll respect every of your traditions." As stupid as they are. "It is absolutely possible to have the church ceremony before the reception in Vaux-le-Vicomte castle."

"Where?"

"In Vaux-le-Vicomte castle built under the reign of Louis the 14th," I inform proudly. She stares at me, surprised. "It's only that, I have already taken care of a few points with our wedding planner. The Vaux-le-Vicomte castle happens to be Louis and I, choice." Mainly mine.

"Haven't you thought of conferring with us?"

Not really.

"I think it is incumbent upon my fiancé and I to make the most important decisions about our wedding ceremony, except, of course, those concerning your traditions, for which I have a deep respect."

"Are you on the pill?"

"I beg your pardon?!"

"It is of the essence that you are, I hope you're aware of it."

"Well…"

"Louis is an only son and a very sensitive young man, do you act upon his needs?"

"I think I am."

"At best, another one will come!"

"I'm sorry, I'm not sure I understand."

"Before you, were Chloe, Carla, Marie, Julie, and Fanny… hasn't he mentioned them?"

"Yes…" Hell no! "… but I'm not getting the point."

"As many relationships that ended with a failure!"

"I doubt being just a fling." There's no way I'm going anywhere. Plan C. "Our encounter was truly love at first sight, it can only be a GODSEND," I say to Satan to burn him.

"And how did it occur?" he probes, curious, glancing at me.

"During a charity gala, in honor of Darfur. Our fight against world hunger has caused it. Is there a more beautiful start for a relationship?" I argue tenderly, to soften her.

"What was the amount of your donation?"

"With all due respect, the question is rather indiscreet. Philanthropic contributions aren't motives of bragging." Especially if the amount is insignificant.

"How then would I check your motivations?"

"Well, my claims are easily verifiable, I was participating in charity galas way before meeting your son." Philanthropy is vital when leading a double life. "Anyway, I doubt you would be able to sense my love for Louis, as it exceeds human comprehension," I assert while suddenly standing.

"Sit down, I told you, Louis is a very sensitive young man, I'm only attempting to preserve him."

"Well, be assured, I see to it too!"

That old demon has exhausted me! It is clear that none of

my words will secure her. I'll remain docile to put on a brave face but the conversation is over. My union to her son is tied up and there's no way she'll untie it!

CHAPTER 23

Saturday, May 6th, 11:00 p.m.

W e're taking off at last.

"My mother adores you!" Louis gushes.

"I'm not so sure," I answer coldly.

"It's a confession she slipped in my ear."

"Did she mention the inquisition she led in the living-room?" A tough questioning that only mothers-in-law hold the secret of. "The number of my donations, my wealth, my savings, the names of my ex's, and even the reason why I was still single before meeting you." Did she think she could intimidate me? She'd never had the foolishness to do that if she knew who I was!

"She just wanted to get to know you."

"By imposing me the pill?"

"I admit that she can be bossy."

"You mean tyrannical?"

"She's just very protective."

"I call that a Œdipus complex!"

Does she also sew his boxers?

"Darling, you're not the only one to have invested my life."

"Before me, there were Chloe, Carla, Marie, Julie, and Fanny… were you planning on telling me about them someday?"

"They were only flings."

"Important enough to have them meet your parents."

"None of them hold a candle to you!"

"Tell that to your mother!"

"She knows it already!"

I reconsider.

"Anyway, what does it matter?" I have more influence on her son that she'll never have! "Come here!" I command, satisfied.

He frowns with surprise.

"Is the storm over?"

"I have a gift for you."

Mathilde brought me the Rolex before dinner. I wrapped it in a golden paper printed with his initials.

"Darling, you shouldn't have!"

"Of course, I should…" In addition to spying on him, I always alternate rewards and spanking. "Open it."

Like a kid on Christmas morning, whose face illuminates when seeing the only toy he doesn't own.

"The GMT-Master II?"

"And since you were late for our last six dates…"

"I admit it's full of subtlety!" he exclaims, his eyes filled with credulity.

"Turn it, I had it engraved."

It's even more subtle.

"Since we're for life?" he asks tenderly.

I nod, Machiavellian, while strapping the Rolex to his wrist as you handcuff a prisoner…

CHAPTER 24

Monday, May 8th, 4:00 p.m.

Things are going well. I'm an influential business-woman engaged to a financial magnate, I own an offshore account in the Bahamas, and today, I have a first appointment, at the Edmond de Rothschild bank, the wealthy people's bank. I make a deposit of a relatively high amount that is for me the work of a lifetime. My rising in the elite is a goal that I haven't stopped pursuing since my primary years and I have climbed the social ladder to conquer the most prestigious positions in society. This day is therefore filled with meaning, the one of a so deserved personal achievement.

The Edmond de Rothschild bank neighbors embassies, high fashion boutiques, and the prestigious art galleries decorating the luxurious *rue du Faubourg-Saint-Honoré*. Its building is bourgeois and its lobby faces a monumental red-carpeted stair in front of which a young assistant is waiting for me, smiling.

"Welcome to Edmond de Rothschild, Miss, please follow me."

We climb the stairs leading to my 4:00 o'clock, as I glance up, I see he's observing me from upstairs. Would he be hopping up and down with impatience to see me?

"Welcome, Baroness."

"Good afternoon, Jacob." Jacob de Rothschild, one of the de Rothschild Clan heirs.

"I am delighted to have you here," he says, shaking my hand.

"The pleasure is all mine."

"Please, come in." He clears me the way and we sit at his magnificent Victorian period antique desk. "May I offer you some refreshments?"

"No, thank you."

I'm much more distracted by the beauty of the place, a vast and bright Napoleonic decor.

"The furniture comes from the Grand Trianon of Versailles," he satisfies himself.

"I know, I was at the auction."

I distill a zest of arrogance to set the tone and his eyes narrow to assess me.

"I read twenty-nine years old on your file and yet I wasn't expecting such a young lady, your alias portends another woman…"

"You probably imagined the portrait of an old botoxed lady?"

"You're reading my mind, why did you choose *The Baroness* as a pseudonym?"

"It perfectly matches my impressive personality."

Which he'll end up realizing.

"Should I call you that?"

"Not necessarily."

"I know how important anonymity is to you, hence my question."

"We're in a private investment bank, I see no inconvenience to the use of my real name."

"I'd rather call you *Baroness.* "

"If you insist."

"I find this alias particularly elegant," he confesses enthusiastically, his head cocked slightly to one side.

"I won't contradict you."

"I admit I have been remarkably surprised by the yearly ascent of your consulting firm. At twenty-nine, it's quite rare to develop such a flourishing business as yours. How did you achieve such success?"

"Word of mouth did its work."

"Do you sell dreams to your clients?"

"I rather make theirs true."

"So, it's not a myth?"

"I'm not."

He fixes me with his blue stare.

"How would you proceed if my wife came to you with infidelity doubts?"

"That's a funny question."

"Why?"

"You're gay."

Oh, his body temperature just went up.

"What lets you assert such a thing?" he asks, flushing red, trying to hide his psychological discomfort by readjusting his chair scores of times.

"It's often said to me that I stink money and power."

"And?"

"You stink poetry: the violin next to the windows, the raspberry-pink socks, the Chanel fruity perfume…"

"That's no more than a set of allegations."

The silk tie, the manicure…

"The list is long and at this stage it's rarely a coincidence."

"Unfortunately, you're wrong."

I'm never wrong.

"You pretend to be married but I see no couple, children or country house pictures."

"What's the point?"

"You're not wearing a wedding ring either."

"I could be divorced."

"You hold no mark of it."

"It's true, I'm still looking for the woman of my life."

"It's rather exceptional that a man your age and condition would still be looking for the woman of his life. Especially if he's from such a conservative family as the Rothschild."

He regards me intently, I have the feeling he just understood.

"You're a fascinating young woman."

"You noticed."

Basic lesson: stun out of your lack of humility, you'll then go from indifference to curiosity.

"Tell me about you, Baroness."

"What do you want to know?"

"You were born in the south of France, you have studied the Human entity for almost a decade, you like golf, and you spend all your summer vacations on yachts off the coast of Saint Barthelemy."

"The essential points are there."

"This ready-made biography doesn't explain your superiority complex or your need to impose it to the world."

"Doesn't it need to be astonished?"

"You like the spotlights?"

"I feel at ease with them."

"Why not broadcast yourself?"

"I value my privacy."

"What are you hiding?"

"Serenity."

"That state of mind is incompatible with your personality!"

He promptly stands, putting an end to the conversation, and heads to the mahogany mini bar from which he takes a whisky bottle out. A long silence suddenly invades us. I take this opportunity to ask myself an existential question: if the fifty-something gay man, who drinks in the middle of the day, can lead such a prestigious bank as the Rothschild's, what about the future of a young woman as brilliant as I am? The answer seems quite obvious and has enough to torment.

"You hold all the characteristics of leaders and I – despite your disinterest for it – have the feeling you could become the one of all women in the world."

"Who's talking about disinterest?"

He comes back to seat with a glass in hand.

"Would you seize the opportunity if a bank such as Edmond de Rothschild could back you up?"

"How would you do that?"

"What would you say about a check with as many zeros as necessary to start the building of a potential empire?"

Are the three glasses of whisky he chugged the source of that tempting offer or is that alcoholic holding a part of rationality that escaped my clarity?

"What would you gain?"

"Ten percent of your fees."

"Develop."

"You could give international conferences, launch your own tv show, invade social media, and present yourself, to the world, as the skillful woman who perfectly masters love and can teach it to anyone."

Maybe he's not as stupid as he looks.

"Only, I'm a business woman, Jacob, not a showgirl."

"You're an absolute cash machine and you don't even

know it!" *Of course, I do, moron!* "Haven't you thought of the multitude of women who could call on your services if they knew of your existence?" Italians living under patriarchal domination, Chinese being crushed under the weight of masculine traditions, Americans getting high on romance movies, and all those sad women that I could take under my tutelage and to whom I would give the keys to happiness. "You could fill entire rooms of feminine troops that you'd galvanize as you wish and you'd become one of the most emblematic figureheads of international feminism, that of which you probably always dreamed." His business proposal just sounds too good to be true. That sneaky will probably end up imposing coercive conditions that will insidiously catch me in a vice. I bet at the end, he'll want me to dance wearing panties on a golden stage, as Beyoncé does. "You're way too silent… do I still need to argue?"

"No need Jacob, I think we've examined the question from all sides."

"Well then, what holds a woman like you from initiating her conquest of the world?" The world conquest would be very fine if it didn't include being bankrolled by a gay capitalist of which horns growing out of his head are as long as his teeth. "You probably prefer remaining under the Beaumonts' feet?"

"I beg your pardon?"

"Congratulations, by the way."

"I've never been anyone's puppet."

"By entering that family, you'll end up being one much faster than you imagine."

"My firm and its financial data speak for me. I managed to build them by myself and under the control of my sole authority. See how independent I am."

"You'll have a difficult time remaining so under the constraints of the Beaumont."

"I doubt we're talking about the same people."

They're so disconnected from reality.

"How do you think they have reached such wealth, if not by enslaving all their environment?" He said either too little or too much. "Haven't you ever wondered why was Louis Beaumont still single when you met him?" I hold his gaze steadily. "Just ask all those who came before you."

"I strongly doubt to be anything like those women."

"I doubt it too and it isn't a coincidence that you stink money and power, you're cut out for that. I'm giving you the opportunity to get what's rightfully yours."

"Let's cut it, please." I take a check out of my handbag. "Here's the deposit to open my account."

"Two million?" He smirks. "A trifle compared to what a collaboration such as ours could produce in terms of numbers!"

"Don't insist, Jacob."

"Good heavens, are you serious?"

"Don't I look like it?"

"Well, take your check back, it's no longer appropriate to open an account today!" Would he actually dare?! "You'll contact me when you're ready to reach the highest levels of this world!"

"Do you think you can throw me out with no consequences?"

"I'm not throwing you out, Baroness, you're most welcome here. However, if our advice isn't satisfactory to you, it is probably smarter to go elsewhere."

I stand.

"You have no idea what I'm capable of!"

"You're certainly the queen of your little world, but at

Rothschild, you're out of your league, here, we make money, not pussyfoot!"

I leave and slam the door; my return will be as noisy.

CHAPTER 25

Monday, May 8th, 8:00 p.m.

"Good evening, beauty."

"Join me in the bathroom."

"What?"

"Do as I say."

Nothing like a good roll in the hay to dilute a feeling of anger.

"Here, now?"

"No, in three months."

"In this restaurant?"

I've seen him less prude.

"Since when it is stopping you?"

"Darling, anywhere but here!"

It would certainly be indecorous to make love in a restaurant where we regularly come but…

"I don't give a damn about protocols!"

"Well I do, we have a reputation to uphold."

"It's precisely the point, actually!"

"Darling, everyone is looking at us, please, sit down."

"I don't want to sit down, I want to fuck!"

The murder envy won't go away that easily.

"Very well, but tell me!"

"That crazy Rothschild threw me out of his bank!" He'll boast quite less when the Paris smart set will be told of his sadomasochistic gay habits!

"Wait, I'am having trouble understanding you…"

I end up sitting, this conversation doesn't seem to be ending.

"I impudently turned away one of his business proposals." And since knowledge is power, I will refrain telling about the warnings he gave me on his family.

"Rothschild made you an offer?"

"Broadcasting myself for his check book."

"Rothschild wanted to fund you?"

"Does it seem so unlikely?"

"But why did you refuse? It's a lifetime opportunity, it's what you always wanted!"

"How do you think it would end? See how he treated me!"

"Darling, he's a capitalist, it's no news to you, we're just like him!"

"That man is so Machiavellian. He would crush me without blinking an eye and gladly use any fault to ruin my reputation."

"Why, do you have something to hide that I don't know about?"

A plethora!

"Sir, Miss, here are your dishes."

Damn, I have never been happier to see a prole! What could I have announced to a man I'm marrying in less than a year, that the life of the woman he idealizes more than anything else is marked by grey areas that will never fade away?

"I can't believe you turned away such an opportunity!" That fool is so naïve! "You could be the woman you always wanted to be and get what you've always worked for."

"I'm already the woman I've always wanted to be and as for wining what I've always worked for, it won't be long."

"And how do you intend to achieve that?"

Your parent's address book will be plenty enough!

"I'll find out," I say innocently. For now, I can't stand that codfish anymore, we're having dinner in this restaurant three times a week and we're always on the same routine: same dishes, same faces, the same table on the terrace close to the landscaped garden… That monotonous symphony will unavoidably lead me to hang myself. "I received a call from New York last week, it could be an amazing opportunity," I say, pretending to be interested.

"You'd want to move there?"

"Why not? I could live my American Dream, spend the winters in Aspen and the summers in the Hamptons."

"We're already having a hard time seeing each other in the same city and you want to move to another continent? What kind of marriage will we be in if you live on the other side of the world?"

"I'm asking you to come not to stay."

"How could I? Half of my clients are in France, the other half is scattered across Europe."

"What does it matter, you'll have new clients in the United States, you'll conquer Wall Street and I, the elite of New York, it'll be a marvelous challenge for both of us."

"Well, I'll pass!" he rebels dangerously.

"Is my fiancé a milksop who can't take risks?"

"Why would I tempt fate while my career is well off here?"

"Because your fiancée commands it!" I roar, to set his ideas straight.

"It's the same for you, your business is doing well, if you

want more, call Rothschild back but don't risk an adventure that would leave you wounded!"

"Are you doubting me?!"

"Be realistic, don't ruin everything!"

"That's what you're doing!"

It's enough! I stand.

"Where are you going?"

I leave as upset as I came. And to think that the New York conversation was only a way to elude my intentions!

CHAPTER 26

Monday, May 8th, 9:30 p.m.

We usually go back together after our dinners. At his place or mine, I always pick the most appropriate option. Tonight, I'm going home, alone and thoughtful. I put my bags next to the entry door, take off my shoes, abandon my trench coat on the sofa, and walk in the long hallway leading to the kitchen. I remember I have a bottle of vodka somewhere in the cupboards. It was a gift from a Russian client I set up with a real estate tycoon. "Forty years old and still not married." It was the subject line of the e-mail she had sent me. That day, Louis had said « I love you » for the first time. After two weeks dating me, he was already wrapped around my finger. He didn't understand how he could have reached that point and I never confessed I was a seduction expert who knew the human entity inside and out. His cerebral system mechanism, his emotions' management, his moves, postures, language, social interactions… he had no shot escaping me.

I found the bottle of vodka. Finally, I won't drink any. I get out on the terrace and light a cigarette. I usually don't smoke but, just as jogging, it sometimes provides release, soothing, and help. I go through my chaotic appointment with

Rothschild and my heated dinner with Louis. My thoughts shove with as much madness as the clashes of the day but I channel my fury and keep rational. It works this way when you're gifted.

CHAPTER 27

Tuesday, May 9th, 9:00 a.m.

"**G**ood morning, Baroness!"

"Good morning, Marie."

"Here's your orange juice, your messages, and your schedule for the day."

"Marie, today I'm there for no one, except for the Cartier boutique manager."

I've ordered a tiara and a diamond ring that perfectly suits my ego.

"I'm sorry Baroness, I haven't included your fiancé's messages. There are thirty-three, do you wish to listen to them?"

My man shouldn't leave so many messages, he should find me, push me against a wall, and grab my lips.

"It's not necessary, archive them." Those modest reconciliation attempts are certainly not suitable for my person. I'll try considering them when he tries a little harder. By the way… "Trace the call we received from New York, I'd like to know where it came from."

That argument only resulted in arousing my curiosity. What if that client could actually be the cause of my ascent to the top? If all that spat was merely a sign to force me calling her back? If it is now or never… how could I make sure of it? I sit at my desk. My head is filled with questions and I stare at the buildings of Paris. They're not as imposing as New York skyscrapers but they instantly deport me there. I foresee that international icon arrogantly setting its hyper-power and I can't help thinking it's made for me.

"Baroness…" Marie bothers, with a high-pitched voice. Helene Beaumont is here for you.

I am taken aback.

What does she want? Finish off her inquisition?

"Bring her in."

Her coming is far from enchanting me but the splendor of my office might help her realize the magnitude of my importance.

Hearing her heals zealously clicking on the wooden floor, I straighten up in my executive chair. My head is high and my hand under my chin when she makes her damned entry, her eyes are piercing and her hair hideously puffed up.

"What a lovely surprise!" I say, smiling broadly to flatter her.

"So, this is the place!" she exclaims while vigorously inspecting every single thing in the room.

My pride multiplies by ten.

"It's indeed here that…"

"You swindle all wealthy men of the city!"

"I beg your pardon?"

"Did you really think I didn't know?" she asks while seating.

"Since we rub shoulders in the same circles, it seemed obvious that some of our mutual friends had mentioned me, on occasions. Did they recommend you to call on my services?" I taunt brazenly.

"I threw your business card into the toilet after urinating."

Her affection never cease to delight me.

"Let me offer you a coffee…" … creamed with Marie's phlegm. "The houses' specialty…" … we give to unfaithful husbands. "It will make our discussions much nicer."

"Don't try to trick me!"

"I wouldn't think of it, but haven't I been clear enough about my activities?"

"You're no more than a white-collar offender, you meddle in married couples' lives to break them and you take the opportunity to grab immense sums of money that you use to maintain your lavish lifestyle, that's what you do!"

"Think again, I make my money in the most legit way."

"Louis is obviously not aware."

"We're both free to manage our businesses as we see fit."

"And that makes it convenient for your scheming!"

"There's nothing illegal in my activities, contracts preside over them and my clients officially appoint me to get in their marriages."

"Do they command you to rob their husbands?"

"It's nothing more than financial compensation."

That contributes, among other things, to pay for my secondary home mortgage on the French Riviera.

"Did you think you could enslave my son with such ease?"

"I told you, I'm in love with him."

"At least as much as I'm in love with my husband!" What's that psycho?! "I should have never let you enter our home!" she claims, her eyes wide open as she stands. "And you'll never come again!"

"Please, don't be…"

"No more than in our family, by the way!"

She really gets on my nerves!

"In case you hadn't noticed, it's already done!"

"Do you think you can marry my son with impunity?"

I raise my eyebrows in surprise.

"Do you really want to bet on that?"

"Very well then, I'll crush you!"

"You obviously don't know me as well as you think."

"No alcohol, no coffee, no weaknesses… you're nothing but a dominatrix deserving a good spanking!"

"And of course, you want to take that in your hands."

"You seem to ignore the immense number of predators I've broken in my life!"

"Would The Baroness be the next one on the list, by any chance?"

"You're not even a real one!"

"I never said I was."

"Of course not, you'd rather ingeniously manipulate people, just as you tried to do with our family." How insightful! "Here you are unmasked! Now, either you leave and keep dignity, money, and business, or you keep wanting to marry my son and I'll destroy you. I'll drag your name through the mud and I will harass you until dementia. You'll lose your firm, your pride, and I won't even spare your girlfriends who will all run away, one after the other!"

My face darkens.

"Let's set things straight. I have never bent under threats, I have never abdicated, I have never given up, I have never backed off from any obstacle. I've built my empire with my sole labor and if I must bury you under my desk to keep it, I won't give it a second thought!" I declare impetuously, as I stand. "It's therefore entirely in your interest to calm down if you want to avoid me calling a few surgeon girlfriends so that they skin you alive and give me your head, that I'll proudly display next to the files of all those wealthy men that I have masterfully lynched!"

"That, we will see!" she asserts as she hastily walks to the door.

"And only come back with the intention to greedily lick my feet, just as your son, my loved one!" I shout, very conscious that the war is officially declared. The door slammed, the tone is set. "Marie, get in the boarding room with Sophie!"

We have now to prevent all possibilities.

I actively cross the hallway leading to the boardroom and I furiously enter in it. My assistants, who are seating around the table, give me a quizzical look.

"We never had a meeting on a Tuesday…" Sophie remarks, surprised.

"The situation requires it," I say in a solemn tone, firmly pressing the seat I'm standing behind. "My mother-in-law just left the firm leaving a huge problem to handle."

"Didn't I tell you marriage is no formality?" she says ironically.

"Spare me your sarcasm, FYI, your job is on the line."

"I thought you weren't closing the business?"

"I have no such intention, but her evil spell could certainly force us to, so switch on your tablet and take notes, if you don't want to end up jobless." She complies and I start a slideshow on the plasma screens. "Here's the deal: Helene Beaumont is threatening to destroy the firm if I don't give up my marriage."

"Since when do you take threats seriously?" she interrupts, looking astonished.

"That demon is worth a hundred million euros and holds an address book as filled as the Queen of England's, so it is in our interest to actually take her threats seriously."

"Why does it matter if our activities are legal?"

"She stressed the unfaithful husbands, she could easily find and convince them to file a class action against me. If they all mention the same version of the story, including blackmailing and false imprisonment, it could be a very big problem."

"Even if they signed a contract?"

"Under the threat of Yuri, who, by the way, has no legal status to act as a bodyguard."

"I thought their offshore accounts were means of pressure that would protect us."

"Not if my mother-in-law's contacts give them amnesty, in which case…"

"We're all…"

"Indeed."

"I never thought it could be so serious."

"I would, therefore, ask you to be involved as much as possible," I intone solemnly, looking at them one after the other.

"We're all affected!" Marie shouts, complacently.

"Given the number of enemies, you're making each second…" Sophie adds.

"It had to happen."

That's why I planned half a million in small bills and a plane waiting on a tarmac, ready to take off for my chosen tropical destination.

"So what do we do now?"

"We must destroy all evidence showing those men at the firm, including and mostly, video recordings of their coming, among which the buildings' and our meetings in my office."

"Did you record your appointments with those guys?" Sophie asks, surprised.

"I'm a dominatrix, what do you think, that I'd don't get a kick out of reviewing my performances?"

"Each to his own little games," she giggles dumbly.

"You like alcohol, I like money and power, understand that between us is a whole world you'll never reach."

"I was joking!"

"I'm not, you'll stay here until we've found all the recordings. We have five years of business, when you get through a year, switch to the next." They sigh. "You're right," I say, nodding. "There are more than a thousand recordings, the day promises to be as long as the night."

"Meaning you stripped more than a thousand men?"

"That is to say a whole army."

Such data isn't unrelated to my narcissism and my superiority complex.

"And how will you justify their bank transfers and the fact that they match the amounts their wives received?"

"I have no link with those financial transactions. They're made on untraceable accounts and the wives receive them through divorce insurance they sign up for when contracting my services. Nothing directly incriminates me, except those video recordings that you'll have to burn outside the city, in the suburbs. After that, we'll attack. I want you to find out anything on that Waco, including the color of her panties and the size of her bra cups. Also get information on Louis' exes, when and why it ended."

"Wait a minute, I also have Louis's case to handle, I can't do everything at once," she grumbles shaking her head."

"GODDAMN, why can't you be as submissive and mute as Marie is?"

"Maybe she doesn't have the same workload."

"You only have two files to handle, if you're overloaded then change jobs!"

"You asked me to put trackers on his suits, there are more than fifty of them, I'm sorry I can't do everything at once."

"Well, leave that aside, we have priorities!" I command, pointing Satan's picture on the plasma screen. "Now, grab boxes in the broom closet and get yourselves in the archives room!" I conclude, vigorously opening the door.

I, myself, head to that 50 square meters room containing the files of my clients, whose lives I've literally transformed and for which the bill is being handed to me now. I have no intention of giving up, but who knows what could occur if all the husbands I've destroyed united together? World War II would certainly look pale compared to that!

CHAPTER 28

Wednesday, May 10th, 6:00 a.m.

The sun rises.

We spent the night at the office. All of us driven by the wish to keep the firm alive and boosted, to achieve that, by protein bars and power drinks of which three-quarters of the stock is gone.

"I'm gonna take a pee break!" Marie shouts as she rushes out of the archives room.

"We all deserved it," I reckon, serene. We found all video recordings and piled them up in boxes ready to be incinerated. "Burn them in Sarcelles district and go home to rest," I order Sophie, whose fatigue adorns the face.

"What about your mother-in-law?"

"You still have to get information on her. We need means of pressure to attack."

"Okay, I'll keep you posted," she replies, jaded.

"For a soldier, you seem to be giving up quite fast, don't you think?" I ask sharply, to remind her of the reason why I recruited her.

"No worries, I'm here."

"And after all this time, you should know that I absolutely don't care about other people's feelings. Yours are no exception to the rule, so, come to your senses," I suggest while leaving the room with disdain.

I have enough problems without her becoming one of them. Louis still didn't bother come to apologize. I go to my office to listen to his voicemails, I can't wait to hear him beg before seeing him grovel.

"Will you end up answering me?" a male voice questions from the back of the lounge.

I quickly turn my head.

"Louis?"

How did he get in?

"The door was open and there was no one at the reception desk, I took advantage of it to sneak in," he explains, casually seated on the sofa. I hang up. "I canceled my business meetings to come to talk to you," he continues, with flattery.

"That's progress," I declare coldly to show I'm still upset with him.

"It's not my only attempt. I called you, I sent you messages, e-mails, I even went to your house yesterday evening but I didn't find you there." That's because women my stature are way too busy setting things straight for those having a hard time figuring out who they're dealing with. "Did you spend the night here with Yuri?" What's does Yuri have to do with it and how does he know? "I was very surprised when my parents' private detective gave me that file."

He points it on the table.

"What is it?" I ask quietly, slowly moving to the sofa.

Probably one of the many devious tricks of his mother's to oust me while keeping her hands clean.

"That's funny, I told myself the same thing. And I precisely came so that you could explain to me why my fiancée, acting as a consultant, requires a bodyguard..." he replies acidly.

Okay, here we go again with drama performances and reverse psychology.

I blink at him innocently and sit on the sofa.

"I'm led to meet with violent husbands having a hard time accepting the advice I give their wives, you wouldn't want your fiancée to fall into a deep coma, would you?"

"Why have you never mentioned it?" he asks staring at me to gauge my reaction.

"Why would I have? Do you talk to me about your work?"

"Interpol has issued an arrest warrant against him, he's wanted for two murders, including that of a cop, did you know that?"

"Of course not."

Of course, I did, if not, what would be the point?

"Perfect, then you'll have no trouble letting him go," he declares as he stands.

What's the fantasy?

"I have no such intention."

I gaze impassively back, not blinking or backing down.

"Did I hear you right?"

I stand.

"Since when do you give me orders?"

"He killed two men, you'll have to get rid of him!"

"Don't tell me how to run my business!"

"GODDAMN, he's a criminal! Imagine what it would do to our family if people knew that my fiancée meddles with organized crime cons!"

"I'm not meddling with him, he's my bodyguard! So yes, he has a history and he looks the part, he's fierce and that's all that matters!"

Our hands wave, the conversation is getting heated.

"Not to me! So, you immediately get rid of him or I will!"

"You've been told off by your mother, right?"

After threatening daughters-in-law, warning the sons, that's what bitches do!

"Leave my mother out of it!"

"Do you really think she has nothing to do with it?"

"She doesn't even know!"

"You neither, apparently!" He stares at me, stunned. Poor thing, he's even more stupid than I thought! "Why do you think I spent the night here? In tears, comforted by my assistants! Well, go on, call your mother and ask her! Ask her why she threatened me! Ask her why she asked me to choose between you and my firm!" He gasps and swallows. I take a deep breath, close my eyes, and run my fingers through my hair. "Anyway, you'll never believe me," I add with a monotone voice, heading to the floor-to-ceiling windows.

He breathes in and walks over to me.

"How am I supposed to take that?"

"Ask your mother!" I say, back turned. "She's the one who wants to split us up!"

"You have to admit that we don't need her to argue, lately."

I turn around.

"Of course, you always see the worst in me! I supposedly want to keep you away from our life together, I'm not brilliant enough to start my firm in New York, and I would even have close ties with the Serbian mafia!"

"You're twisting my words, that's not what I said!"

"All the same!"

"But you're so secretive and everything is so complicated with you! I couldn't explain to my mother what your real job is, since I don't even know what you do!"

"As if it mattered to you!"

"Much more than you think!"

"Oh stop it, you deal with millions, I with thousands, I know how derisory and insignificant you think my business is, compared to yours!"

"You're completely mistaking!"

"You know very well I'm right! If it wasn't the case, you'd have no trouble coming with me to New York!"

"But since when do men vanish for women?"

Since forever, dummy!

"And macho, now!"

"Listen, I didn't come here to fight."

"Allow me to doubt that!"

"I just wanted…"

"To apologize?" I ask with a calm and emotionless voice.

"Let's stop hurting each other."

"Do the honors, start with respecting your fiancée and trusting her," I suggest as I look at his fixed Rolex. "Because our marriage won't last long, if you have, for me, the littlest atom of suspicion or contempt."

"Rest assured, we'll be happy," he asserts as he comes closer.

"It's an awful start, though."

"You have to do your share because I too need trust and respect."

"I always gave you that."

In appearance, at least.

"I was really furious when I heard about that Yuri character." It's rather a relief, as far as I'm concerned. One less secret isn't negligible data. "I thought you pushed me away again."

"I never have."

And will always do.

"Then, take my opinion into account and get rid of him."

I clench my fists. He can dream on!

"Very well, give me the time to find a replacement." Or

rather, to marry you with joined ownership. "Then, I'll tell you what you want to hear." That's he's just a scatterbrained, doubled with a daddy's boy, who's only good to squander his parents' money.

"And I will talk to my mother." Good dog, sit, down. "But I know she likes you."

"Are you trying to comfort me or rather to protect her?"

He caresses my cheek with his fingertips.

"She loves you as much as me…" he declares, looking at my lips.

"Well then, what are you waiting for to kiss me?"

My kisses never ended to soothe him. That's what allows me to think that I'll always have more power over him than his bitchy mother will ever have!

CHAPTER 29

Thursday, May 25th, 8:00 a.m.

Fifteen days have gone since my argument with Louis. His mother denied threatening me, pretending it was a misunderstanding and I took advantage of her retreat to multiply make-up sex. This morning, I leave his bed to go to the office. Everything his back into place, there's no reason to fake it anymore.

I take my bags when he walks out of the bathroom, naked torso, towel around the hips. His skin is glistening and he has a stubble beard.

"May I have a last kiss before you go?" he whispers into my ear as he embraces me from behind. I lean my head, give him a long lingering kiss, and run my hand through his damp hair.

"That's all I needed to start my day right," I pretend, staring at him.

"I don't want to leave you."

"We have to go back to work."

"You're right, don't forget Yuri…"

"Louis, we've already talked about it."

"I know, I just wanted to remind you."

"Trust me, you have nothing to worry about."

"Very well, I'll let you leave. I have to go as well, pack my suitcase and organize files."

"Where are you going?" I ask mischievously, although I'm perfectly aware.

Sophie wrapped up his case, he can't hide anything from me anymore.

"To Berlin, in two hours," he answers naïvely.

"We'll meet for dinner?" In the same restaurant, with the same dishes, the same faces, the same table on the terrace close to the same landscaped garden.

"As usual!" he gushes stupidly.

I walk to the door and come back.

"Before I leave…"

I put my hands on his chest and give him one last kiss to mark his spirit with my presence and better tie him up.

CHAPTER 30

Thursday, May 25th, 9:00 a.m.

"Good morning, Baroness!"

"Good morning, Marie."

"Here's your orange juice, your messages, and your schedule for the day."

"I'm listening, Marie."

"I put on your desk the new infidelity files, you have *84* appointment requests, Sophie is in your office regarding the Helene Beaumont case, Sarah Baywood sent you new *3D* visualizations, she confirms that Ed Sheeran is booked and she'd like you to call her back about the fireworks you mentioned."

"Fine." All is consistent with my wishes, again. I rapturously open the office door. Sophie is seated on the sofa, legs crossed lying on the table. "Make yourself at home!" She jumps.

"I thought you wouldn't come."

"Why is that?"

"You took two weeks off."

"I told you, things have to be prioritized. As a matter of fact, I killed two birds with one stone, by saving my wedding, I'm saving the firm and your job by the way, don't thank me, it's my pleasure." I sit at my desk. "Come here and tell me what you found out on the old psycho."

"Baroness, your tax advisor is on the line."

I look at my watch.

"Not now." We'll have lunch at *Fouquet's*, we'll have plenty of time to giggle.

"Very well, Baroness."

Sophie sits and puts a file on the desk.

"Here's what you wanted."

"Talk to me about Louis'exes, first," I order as I switch on my Mac.

"Two of them are in psychiatric hospitals, the three others almost got committed. Your mother-in-law always uses the same method: she threatens, she blackmails, and she sucks everything to the last dime."

"Aren't those girls prominent, from wealthy families?"

"That she shatters through scandals until they're bankrupt."

"Interesting..." I murmur while looking at the last 3D visualizations. I send an e-mail to Sarah Baywood to confirm them. I smile radiantly, my wedding promises to be as dreamy as can be. "Did you talk to them?" I continue, the eyes wandering between the screen and the keyboard.

"I met with three of them, they're terrified. Your mother-in-law traumatized them. You're right, this time, we have to be cautious. She destroys anyone willing to approach their clan and assets."

"Are you saying they marry among themselves to protect their lineage, as those degenerated freemasons?"

"And the worst part is that I didn't find anything to thwart her. Aside from a nutmeg intolerance but perhaps it won't interest you."

"Then, why that big file?"

"That's the list of all those she ousted."

"Explain to me what are you paid for if you're not capable of providing answers?"

"I'm sorry but I haven't found anything because she doesn't leave anything behind. That woman is a fucking conjurer, she even uses doppelgänger to protect herself."

"So, you're saying I have no way to hit back?"

"But you can protect yourself."

"Then you'd better go back on the field and bring me a good reason not to fire you!" I tell, firmly, to boost her.

"B., it's no joke, I haven't found anything!" she claims, her eyes wide, while she opens the file. "I tried everything, look at the report and my methods, she has no archives, no prints, no file, even trackers and wiretapping led me nowhere."

"Baroness, your tax advisor is on the line," Marie interrupts again. How in the hell did I deserve such stupid assistants?! I wonder with a tense expression. "She says it's an emergency."

"I really hope for your sake it is!" I roar as I grab the phone. "Chloe?"

"B., I'm sorry to bother you. It's an emergency, the financial police want your head."

"If it was only them!"

"It's serious, B.,"

It sounds to me, from her tone.

"Just reassure me about one thing…"

"Don't worry, your offshore account is untraceable, however, check all your files, they're on their way to search your office."

"You can't come in! You can't come in!" Marie exclaims while pushing a pack of people trying to penetrate my office.

Sophie stands with horror.

"Chloe, got to go, they're here!"

I feel like I'm dreaming.

Marie is thrown on the floor and the office is suddenly filled with policemen whose rage and impetuosity only equal those of toreros entering the arena.

"Gentlemen, I'm the firm director, how may I help you?" I ask quietly to tame them.

They all surround my desk, as another one slowly steps closer.

Black trench coat, square jaws, impassive face, and austere look.

He places his briefcase on my desk and takes papers out to hand them to me.

"Miss, we have a search warrant and that procedure takes place in the framework of two preliminary investigations you're under: the first about tax avoidance, the second, illegal employment of a criminal wanted by Interpol, who goes by the name of Yuri Yacoskov."

"Marie, call my lawyer," I order firmly, while I'm reading the document.

It's been signed by a judge I don't know but she certainly has ties with Louis' mother. We're going to end the farce quite fast.

"No call before the end of the procedure," Jaws declares sharply, pointing Marie, who immediately stops her sprint. I look at him with contempt, does he really think he can intimidate me? "Your phone and your computer will be temporarily requisitioned," he adds as he successively grabs them from the desk they're on.

"You can't take them, they're work tools I use for my activities."

"Reread the document," he imposes while putting them

in sealed bags. We have every right, including the right to keep you in the premises until the end of the search.

My assistants watch the scene, flabbergasted. They stand next to the office, waiting for instructions I'm unfortunately unable to give.

I'm as powerless as they are, and just as they, I can only endure those reckless men who seem to be backed up by a superior authority against which I can momentarily not fight.

"Where is your bookkeeping?" Jaws asks as he walks to the door to find it.

"It's all digitized," I reply briefly, following him to better spy on him.

My assistants follow me and all the policemen spread in the office. Those bearing guns keep the entry door, the others rush into the archives room, the board room, the wardrobe, Marie's office, and Sophie's. No room is spared, not even the bathroom and the broom closet.

"We're going to film everything, take cameras," I order to my assistants, while I bustle in each room to better grasp the situation. The cupboards are violently opened, clients' files are meticulously examined, my trench coats and my suits are dragged out of the wardrobe for better searching, and Jaws enumerates and seals, frantically, all our surveillance devices. "I have administrative licenses for their use," I explain spontaneously. "And why are you taking them? How could they be connected to potential tax avoidance?" I ask innocently, perfectly knowing I'm being reproached to be linked with Yuri.

Nothing helps. He remains cold and mute, as the other policemen vigorously working to find an incriminating piece of evidence against me. In vain, they will soon leave as empty-handed as they came. And although I am, in a way, very honored that such a deployment is dedicated to me, I also feel very worried at the idea that my clients could find out that a police operation has been conducted in my firm.

The Parisian upper-class is gathered in a very small perimeter and its reputation is only hanging by a thread, a call, a gossip, a piece of information slipping away. What would happen if my clients heard about the suspicions falling on me, or worse if they knew that their files, supposedly confidential, had been opened, photographed, and sealed? I wouldn't give much for my skin if the incident became public. Which could very well happen.

A client should come soon. She'll stay at the entry door without understanding why it's locked. Not to mention the four other appointments of the day that I won't be able to attend either. The telephone won't stop ringing, e-mail notifications come in by thousands. I look at my sealed phone that won't stop working, I think about Louis who probably ringed me, but I can only try to resign myself. I go to my office and nonchalantly seat on the sofa. I look around and realize that I'm, in a way, imprisoned. How ironic when thinking about the thousand unfaithful husbands that I, myself, have detained, threatening them of bringing them to justice for the same tax evasion that I too have operated.

A forced laugh stands on my face. The wheel of fortune seems to have turned.

"I've put the camera on a tripod," Sophie informs as she suddenly appears in my office.

"It's no time to give up, go back to watch them, you never know what could happen," I declare calmly, and in spite of all things, clearly determined to fight.

"They've been here for six hours, we can rest a bit."

"Who says you can stroll?"

"What else can I do?" she growls, throwing herself on the sofa.

"You see, that's why I asked you to dig, we could have avoided that if you'd done your job properly!"

"Are you going to blame me?"

"You bet I am! Whose fault is it if we're unable to anticipate?"

"I told you, I didn't find anything, so maybe you should cut your losses."

"What do you want me to do? Cowardly give up my fiancé?"

"Why does it matter? You're not even in love with him, so keep at least your company, out of pride."

"I doubt that a seduction expert would learn something from a divorced alcoholic who never could sustain an actual relationship with a man!" I say loudly, with a sharp look. A silence settles in. She flushes scarlet. The tension is palpable. "That someone like Marie would be on edge in such a context is highly understandable, but not you, a soldier, trained for endurance, effort, and respect for hierarchy," I lecture, with vigor and craftiness.

"I'm sorry," she concedes, not daring look at me.

"Your apology will only take effect when you show a bit more deference."

"I will."

"Then, take something to note. You'll give a copy to Marie as soon as the search is over."

"Ladies, it's time for us to split," Jaws interrupts while quickly heading my way.

"So, what have we found?" I say ironically as I stand up.

"That's the inventory of all we've taken," he replies, signing a sheet of paper on which a list is scribbled : my MacBook, my iPhone, our surveillance devices, and the investigation file about Louis' mother. Enough to persuade me that the extent of the search and its staging indeed constitute a personal message from *Satan*, who wants to crush me. "Your attorney will keep you informed of the progress of your case," Jaws concludes as he leaves my office with his army.

I go to the door to better appreciate their leaving and simply turn back when it closes.

No hostility, anger or invective.

No anxiety, worry or irritability.

"What's going to happen?" Sophie asks, pensively.

"The procedure hasn't been respected, we'll be able to object," I exult as I take a few notes for my attorney when Marie comes into my office to find out more.

"How do you know it?" Sophie continues, frowning.

"They didn't have me sign their report and that is an obligation set by article 57 of the Penal Code. The procedure will be canceled if we plead it's flawed."

"It won't go further?"

"Anyway, they won't find anything on Yuri, whose existence cannot be found in any document and the potential evidence of tax evasion is nowhere either. In short, it won't go further than Louis and the upper-class women's ears, but it would be plenty enough to ruin my marriage and my business."

"Do you think it comes from Louis' mother?"

"Who else would be able to set up such a wide operation in such a short time?" I say, pacing back and forth, hands on my hips.

"How does she know all that?"

"Her private detective must have tracked us."

"Maybe we should kill her…"

"I thought about it, too."

"Nutmeg isn't necessarily a bad idea."

"But it would be too complicated. Rather start an audit on our servers and electronic devices, look for spyware and phishing programs. Marie, call today's clients, pretend we have a water damage issue and postpone all appointments of the week. You will, then, call our attorney and send her the list of seals. In the meantime, go to an Apple store to replace them."

I put my trench coat on and go find Louis before his mother does.

CHAPTER 31

Thursday, May 25th, 5:00 p.m.

I'm in my convertible, on the way to his office. He always makes a stop there when he returns from a business trip. Those to Berlin, namely, usually don't last longer than a day. He meets a few clients and to my great displeasure, comes back in time for dinner. I don't need to track him to know those details. After two years as a couple, one obviously ends up grasping a partner. His weaknesses, qualities, habits, and flaws are known. The ones to be used to enslave, dominate, and trick him. I press down on the accelerator. I won't let his mother ruin everything.

The subtlety with which I handle sensitive matters has no comparison. It considerably serves my interests and ensures, among other things, the continuity of our relationship. As evidence, he always obeys my orders, never takes a decision without my consent, and the numeric file I secretly keep updated can widely show it. It holds data on all that relates to our love life: the number of text messages, calls, gifts, kisses, or sweet words exchanged, which allows me to evaluate his interest for me on a daily basis. It all followed, not long ago, an exponential growth curve but it seems that we've reached a sort of peak that doesn't leave me indifferent.

I press down on the accelerator.

It is out of the question that our relationship declines. It took me so much time to develop a plan that would result in a well-oiled mechanism for both of us. To me, it's an entrepreneurial project and I won't let my investment end in failure. I almost get there to gag him and I'm more determined than ever.

I never wondered if my actions matched any morality. In the matter of seduction, the end justifies the means. Attracting people can only happen via a multitude of strategies and tricks. I always used that behavior for all I desired: money, power, business, friends, and Louis. I can hardly believe that all I managed to build could suddenly crash, because of a troublemaker that I, ironically, would have overlooked. In that matter, Louis' mother. How could I flout such important data? Her words and actions were so clearly unveiling her intentions. And her personality and the subtle ways she uses to stand out in high society circles are so similar to mine. How could I not see, in her, the praying mantis that I am?

I press down on the accelerator.

Sophie is right, nutmeg might not be such a bad idea…

CHAPTER 32

Thursday, May 25th, 6:00 p.m.

Louis and I work each in an opposite part of the city. It's a personal choice. I chose my workplace according to his. The less I'd see him, the less my mental balance would be affected. It's just that, faking love isn't always that easy and it's even more frustrating when you daily teach it without ever having experienced it. I, therefore, make sure to avoid him and the hour-long drive between our offices seems highly justified to me.

I'm there. His office is ideally located in a very large Haussmann-style building. I park my car next to his. A Porsche that matches mine. The kind of details that remind me, again and again, one of the main reasons for which I picked him: we form an idyllic couple and to me that's priceless.

I step out of the car and cross a vast courtyard enhanced with French gardens. I'm wearing sunglasses and I'm dressed in black, I'm about to play the part of the grieving widow, the part of a woman who would have violently been deprived of her loved one.

"I'd like to see Louis Beaumont," I say calmly to the

indolent hostess, seating behind a huge solid wood desk in the lobby.

"Who's asking?" she replies curiously, staring at me.

"His fiancée."

"One moment, please." She probably phones Louis' new assistant, the Ugly Betty I had hired to replace the D cup bombshell. "His office is on the last floor and the elevator is on your left," our lazybones stupidly informs as she hangs up.

"Do I have to remind you that I am his fiancée?" I ask harshly. "I knew the premises long before your arrival and it is not unlikely that your leaving will be a bit anticipated."

"I'm sorry Miss, I just thought…"

"When having two neurons, don't attempt to think," I conclude curtly as I go to the elevator.

I'm in no mood, right now. My main concern is to figure out how I'm going to get myself out of the situation Louis' mother put me in. The rumor has probably spread and if not, his mother certainly informed him. I step in the elevator, glasses on my nose, and closed fists in my trench coat. I willingly hide my anger and apprehension. A situation can always be controlled as long as you handle emotions. Plus, showing your weaknesses never was a solution. It's rather a good way of drowning into a quagmire. People always use our flaws to crush us, why show them?

The elevators' doors open slowly.

Ugly Betty approaches me in a hurry. I scrupulously stare at her. She is, undoubtedly, scarily ugly but still remains groomed, her black suit jacket is perfectly tailored and her shirt is immaculate white.

"Mrs. Beaumont, may I take your trench coat?"

"It won't be necessary," I say, satisfied though paradoxically embarrassed. I like my future spouse name but I don't forget that Louis' mother is wildly busy taking it away from me.

"May I offer you some refreshment?" Betty offers affably.

"Still water will be fine."

"Hurry up!" she commands her colleague in a stern voice. The last, as ugly as the first, scurries to a door, on the other side of the foyer. "Apologies, Mrs. Beaumont, this way, please."

We take the small hallway.

She opens the office door for me and furtively leaves, smiling kindly.

I enter with a rapid pace.

Louis has his back turned, he's wearing a black suit and polished shoes. His outfit still matches mine. I smile crookedly and my eyes twirl around to take stock of the situation. I'm also glad to see that the decoration hasn't changed, I took care of it: wooden floors, moldings, white walnut wood designer desk, and latest trends art pieces. It's all in the image of my office, very classy and yet very contemporary.

" You never answer my calls but this time, you came," Louis notices without turning back.

His detached voice sounds to reflect a hint of irritability. I make cautious steps on a minefield.

"I have no phone anymore, haven't you heard?"

"All the city has."

That's what I thought.

"Your mother took care of that." And of him, at the same time.

"Here we go again?" he reproaches as he abruptly turns around, hands in his pockets.

"And as usual, you don't seem to be aware," I taunt him as I sit.

I slowly take off my black sunglasses, put them on his desk, lean my head, and cross my legs, *Basic Instinct* way. That's how much I know my classics.

"So, tell me… what don't I know?"

"Many things, believe me," I say with a mastered and quiet voice.

"Do you still have secrets?"

"I was talking about your mother."

"And I'm talking about your little secrets."

I raise my head to gaze at him. I am upset and my calmness shortly transforms into impulsiveness.

"FYI, I'm the one being searched and humiliated! But please hide your empathy for your fiancée, it's irrelevant!"

"If you didn't do anything wrong, it wouldn't have happened!"

"Since when are searches unquestionable proof of guilt?"

"In any case, there are strong presumptions!"

"Has your mother manipulated you again?"

"I can't stand those secrets anymore! Yuri, the search warrant, the offshore account, and my parents' detective just informed me that your profession mainly consists of fleecing powerful men of the city!"

"Those are merely compensations."

"Are they legal?"

"Of course, what do you think, everything is approved by judges, attorneys, legal experts."

"That you know and bribe!"

"You're doubting me again?"

"Don't change the subject!"

"It's not true and you know damn well! They don't take any bribes!"

"You play golf with those women, you have dinner with

them, you celebrate with them, GODDAMN IT, haven't you ever figured there could be a conflict of interest?"

Someone knocks at the door: Ugly Betty is bringing my water.

She puts it on the desk and furtively disappears.

A short interruption that lets me take my emotions in hand back, I'm caught off-guard, his nutty mother attacks on all fronts. The only way to get around it is to claim my innocence and to play the incredulity card. As I always did.

"Or maybe you're doing that on purpose? Shenanigans are part of your nature and personality?" Louis concludes, bluntly.

"Please don't let your mother ruin it all."

"I'd say she's making me face the truth."

"Is that really what you think?"

"You've been lying since the beginning of this relationship."

He stiffens. His mouth presses into a hard-line and his green eyes glittering with anger.

"You're completely raving!"

"So, you didn't do anything wrong?"

"If handling a company in the atypical way I do is a crime, then I'm guilty as charged. I'm guilty of transforming the lives of thousands of women by saving them from their husbands' claws and by giving them what they're entitled to: financial compensation going far above what justice is able to give. And if that makes me a criminal, then fine!"

"That doesn't explain your offshore account or even those suspicious behaviors you have, and all those secrets that I discover in time. We're getting married in less than a year and I don't even know who you are!"

"Is that what your mother convinced you of?"

"Will you stop with that?"

"As she did for all those before me: Chloe, Carla, Marie, Julie, and Fanny? Haven't you ever wondered why your exes ran away?"

"Because they all had a lot of secrets and skeletons in the closet!"

"You're far from the truth."

"I thought it would be different with you."

"It is and you don't even see it!"

"But please, enlighten me."

"I've reached that point because your mother asked me to choose between you and my firm, which you already know, we've talked about it. You may refuse to believe it, but I refused to lose you and that's the reason why I'm being punished. My love for you got me the falling of my firm, my honor, and dignity. I chose you over all I have and all I've built is going away because I refuse to leave you! And just tell me how can I do that if my love for you is stronger than all those fucking nonsense financial matters?"

The bigger the object of desire, the bigger involvement to get it. This guy is worth a hundred million and just for that, I'd have both my arms chopped.

"Understand me…" he whispers as he tilts his head.

"It's always about you! But don't you realize I've come for comfort with my fiancé and instead of that, I'm even more tarnished and humiliated?"

He runs his hand on his mouth and blushes, here is he embarrassed.

I look away, frowning, to remember… how do actresses raise the emotional temperature? I need a small climax to leave.

"I didn't mean to offend you."

He seems confused and shaken.

It's a real child's play now!

"I'd better leave, obviously, I don't belong here," I grumble with a sad face.

"B., please!"

I rush to the door and leave before he has time to stop me.

Let's have him marinate.

I head to the spa to get a massage. The day has exhausted me.

CHAPTER 33

Friday, May 26th, 9:00 a.m.

"Good morning, Baroness"

"Good morning, Marie."

"Here's your orange juice and your messages."

"I'm listening, Marie."

"Eighteen clients have canceled their appointments, thirty-three want more information about their files' confidentiality, your attorney would like you to call her back, I put your new laptop and smartphone on your desk, I downloaded your clients' files, your contracts, your accounting, your schedule, and your mailboxes. Furthermore, your fiancé called, he had white roses delivered that I took the liberty to put in your office and your mother-in-law had black roses delivered that I took the liberty to throw away. Finally, as you can see, everything has been rearranged according to your wishes," she declares enthusiastically.

"Bring me caffeine."

The day promises to be busy.

"B.!" Sophie shouts as I enter the office. "Have you heard? The rumor spread, the clients are already canceling their appointments, we'll lose them all if things go on…"

"It's already done," I say to scare her as I slam the door in her face.

It will certainly take any ironic spirit out of her.

As for me, I don't know what will happen but I always fall back on my feet. At best, the storm will be a short one, at the worst, I can always go abroad, there's always that plane waiting on the tarmac, ready to take off.

"Here's your coffee," Marie murmurs as she delicately puts it on my desk.

"Pass me through Laura Simon," I command while looking at Louis' roses.

There's a card, on which he shares his love and regrets.

His impudence won't have lasted long, but how could I live with the idea that my fiancé is an emotional sissy, unable of tenacity? That fool docilely wanders between his mother's reproaches and his fiancé's manipulations. He has no character and any dominatrix, worthy of the name, could literally break him. The circumstances might be what they are, I will never be reluctant to take care of it.

"Baroness, your attorney is on the line."

I pick up.

"Laura, please, tell me something I don't know."

"I have great news, the procedure is marred by irregularities, I contested the basis of it, there will be no charges against you, and you'll get your belongings back next week."

"Will you be able to get damages?"

"We'll just have to pretend that your reputation was tarnished."

"There's something like it, actually. Some clients have already canceled their appointments."

"Are you worried about what's to come?"

"Not really, no."

"In the end, nobody really knows what happened."

"I also doubt that I'll lose my firm for so little." I run the show. I have as many men at my feet as I have women at my door. "Those afraid of being involved will soon be reassured when they see me strutting in galas, dressed in Versace." I smile broadly. An idea suddenly crosses my mind. "You know what?"

"What don't I know?"

"My popularity ratings will skyrocket after this incident!"

"What's your plan?"

"We'll talk about it when I get back," I claim as I hang up. It all seems so obvious now. "Marie, come to my office with Sophie!"

Why didn't I think of it sooner?

I stand up quickly, I can't stay put, the excitement is at its peak.

"What's going on?" Sophie asks.

"Marie, were you able to trace the call from New York?"

"It came from the City Hall."

A politician?!

"What's with New York?"

"I received a call from a potential client. I hadn't made any decision, now I have an answer. " All that fuss had the merit of comforting me

"What do you know about that New Yorker?"

"I know enough to embark upon a sudden departure! She works at the City Hall and must have a full bunch of wealthy girlfriends, who are only waiting for me to spend a fortune!"

"You want to go to New York now, with all the clients canceling their appointments and all the commotion that goes with it?!"

"The time has never been more appropriate and the

subterfuge is relevant: we're leaving to seize a business opportunity, we spread the news, we come back with a prestigious address book, I increase my firm's reputation, as well as my fees." And I don't give much for Louis' mind when he learns his fiancée left without further notice.

"And what about the ongoing files?"

"We delegate, we refund... what does it matter, we'll figure it out!" What's with the long faces? "What's the problem?" Certainly not their private lives, they don't have one. The first is a spinster, the second a rooted adventurer. "I would appreciate that my team doesn't arrogantly question a decision that already took me a lot to make!"

"I'm with you, Baroness!" Marie exclaims.

What about Sophie's level of commitment, as she's been looking at me for several long minutes without saying a word?

"You know very well that my suitcase is already packed!"

"That's what I wanted to hear!" Now, let's get to it! "Marie, book three business class tickets on the next flight to New York, a black Range Rover waiting at the airport, and a room at the Four Seasons for each of us." It's said then! "The Baroness goes to New York!"

To be continued...